JARED'S PROMISE

BARBARA MCMAHON

Jared's Promise
Copyright © 2018 Barbara McMahon
All Rights Reserved

Chapter One

There was no doubt about it—he'd left the hospital too early.

Jared Montgomery wedged the wooden crutches into the corner of the stair riser, took a breath and lunged up another step. The impact when he landed rocked through his body. Gritting his teeth against the pain, he paused a moment to gather his reserves.

Eyeing the remaining stairs, he counted fourteen. Slowly repositioning his crutches, he took a breath and moved up one more step. His broken ankle throbbed, his good leg burned with the unaccustomed double duty, every bone in his body ached, especially his ribs. Not broken, just bruised. He couldn't tell the difference.

Another step gained.

The door at the left of the landing opened and an inquisitive face surrounded by fluffy white hair peeped out. Mrs. Eugenia Giraux. She'd been his neighbor for the eight years he'd rented his apartment. He couldn't remember speaking with her more than about a dozen times in those eight years.

"Oh, dear," she said, taking a good look at Jared.

He tried to smile, but it hurt too much. At least the

swelling around his eye had diminished. He could clearly see her look of shock.

"Mrs. Giraux," he said. She set great store with manners, but he was too tired tonight to care.

"Oh dear," she repeated, darting across the landing and rapping quickly on the other door.

Jared lurched up again. He hadn't come five thousand miles to be stopped by another eleven steps. He'd make it to the top or die trying.

Bad comparison, he thought grimly as he gathered his strength for another step. He'd barely escaped death ten days ago. No tempting it now.

The second door—his door—opened and a tall blonde woman stepped out, peering down at him in startled surprise.

Glad to stop for a moment, his gaze moved from the top of her head to trail slowly down her body. Tall and shapely with shorts that should be declared indecent, she had long tanned legs that made him forget every ache and pain. Sparks of awareness shimmered in the air. Every nerve ending tingled with unexpected tension. Pricks of excitement and vague yearnings danced across his skin. Banged up and in pain, he still could appreciate a beautiful woman.

Swallowing hard, Jared knew he couldn't blame the pain medication for his reaction—he hadn't taken any since starting out yesterday morning. Maybe he could blame his celibate months while at the oil well site.

"Mr. Montgomery is here," Mrs. Giraux announced needlessly.

Great, just what he needed, two women to watch his every move as he struggled up the steep stairs. It was bad enough to take so long with the cab driver behind him. He didn't need an expanded audience.

"Jared Montgomery?" the blonde asked.

"Who else in their right mind would try to climb these stairs in this condition?" he snapped, clenching his teeth once again against the pain that wracked his body. As soon as he reached the apartment, as soon as he turned over the baby to the woman his sister had hired to care for her, he'd pop a couple of the pain pills the doctor had prescribed and find oblivion in sleep. His headache was growing worse, a lingering result of the concussion. And maybe his jarring climb of stairs. His ribs now felt like a fiery band encircling his body.

"Are you the nurse?" he asked using it as an excuse to hold off on another step.

She licked her lips and heat swirled around him. It wasn't enough that the outside temperature hovered in the high eighties, his own skin seemed to ignite from within. A fever? He drew in another ragged breath. He stared up at her, unable to look away—imagining her silky hair tangled in his hands, her tempting lips rosy from his kiss.

Maybe that concussion had been more serious that he thought!

"I'm not a nurse. Do you need one?" Glancing at the fading bruises on his face, at the cast that covered his foot and leg to his knee, she looked worried.

"Not for me, for the baby," he said impatiently, gesturing behind him.

For the first time, the woman looked beyond him and noticed the cab driver. The bundle he carried awkwardly was an infant in a baby carrier—the sole reason for her presence in New Orleans.

"I'm Jenny Stratford. I'm not a nurse, but I know how to

take care of babies. Your sister hired me."

"I assumed as much, since you obviously have the key to my apartment."

He had ten more steps. He could do that. He'd survived worse. He could make ten more steps.

"Can I help?" Jenny asked, apparently intent on ignoring his bad attitude.

Jared rested against the crutches and stared up at her. Unable to resist, he again let his gaze travel from the pale champagne-blond hair down the slim body . She wore a skimpy sleeveless shirt and those blasted shorts. He could come up with some ideas about how she might help, but they didn't involve getting him up the stairs.

Shaking his head, he gripped the crutches tighter. "Just what do you propose?"

She shrugged, a slow smile starting. "Nothing, I guess. You're almost at the top," she offered encouragingly.

"I can see that." Again he positioned the crutches and hopped up another step. Again the impact slammed through him with the force of an explosion.

Not quite. He'd never forget the effects of a true explosion. Or the results.

"Oh dear," Mrs. Giraux said, watching him with worry in her eyes.

"Mrs. G., I'm sure Mr. Montgomery will make it fine. Thanks for letting me know he was here. I'll see you in the morning." Jenny patted the elderly woman on the shoulder and gently turned her toward her door.

Jared said nothing but appreciated the younger woman's actions in getting rid of his neighbor. At least that made one fewer spectator watching him struggle up the stairs. It would be too much to hope that Jenny Stratford would also disappear—at least until he reached the landing.

He didn't care if it was sheer masculine pride, but he hated anyone seeing him struggle.

Another two minutes and he was down to three remaining steps.

"I drove down this afternoon, but I didn't expect you before tomorrow," she said, stepping back to the doorway, to clear the landing.

"I sent Patti a cable." Another jump and he'd be there. Level surfaces he could manage. But there was no way he'd be able to climb the stairs inside his apartment. Not tonight. Why he had to have a two-story apartment with no elevator was beyond him. Of course normally he loved it when he was home. Now the mere thought of climbing another seventeen steps was more than he could cope with.

He'd crash on the sofa tonight and worry about getting up to his room tomorrow. There was a small half bath beneath the inside stairs for immediate needs. He was too tired to worry about a shower or anything except getting off his feet! Or, rather, foot.

Reaching the landing at last, Jared moved into his apartment and headed directly for the large, overstuffed sofa placed against one wall.

Sinking down gratefully, he lowered the crutches to the floor and leaned back. He was so blasted tired. What didn't ache from the injuries received during the explosion ached from using crutches and sheer exhaustion from the twenty-seven hours of traveling.

Soft jazz melodies floated in through the open French doors, the laughter of tourists faintly discernable in the distance. During the day, Jackson Square bustled with activity, but at night it grew quiet, as if lingering over memories of long ago days—of the Creoles who had called New Orleans home, of the changes the old city had seen over the years. The square had been spared during Katrina, to continue on with jazz playing nearby and the Mississippi flowing by as it had for ages.

It was familiar and welcomed. Jared sighed. Despite the circumstances, it was good to be home.

Jenny switched on another light as the cab driver entered the apartment and carefully placed the infant carrier on the floor. The baby was sound asleep.

"I'll get the bags," he said and turned to head back outside.

Jenny looked at the baby, then back at the man now leaning back on the sofa as if he'd never move again.

He couldn't be more than thirty or thirty-one—and he was drop-dead gorgeous. His sister hadn't mentioned that part. Thick dark hair glinted beneath the light without a speck of grey. His skin was tanned a deep copper, from his hours in the Middle Eastern sun, no doubt. His shoulders and arms were muscular, which explained the ease with which he maneuvered the crutches on the steep stairs. Bruises on the left side of his face were already starting to fade. She bet the trip home had been arduous and tiring.

Suddenly he opened his eyes and looked at her. For the space of a minute, Jenny could neither move nor speak. Trapped by the force of his gaze, she could only stare back, feeling her heart race, her breath catch. His eyes were as blue as her own, the light color a surprising contrast to the dark hue of his skin and hair. The contours of his face seemed carved from teak, from his strong nose to the high cheekbones, to the stubborn jut of his jaw.

When his gaze moved from her eyes to once again skim down her body, Jenny resisted the urge to dash out onto the landing and slam the door between them. She hadn't felt so conscious of her own femininity before. But one look from him, and she started thinking things she had no business thinking.

A million thoughts crowded her mind. She wasn't ready for his arrival. She hadn't unpacked, hadn't bought groceries or aired out the apartment or made the beds with fresh linens. She still wore shorts from her drive down, had done nothing with her hair since that morning. And on top of all the thoughts that tried for dominance was the glaring one that concerned her more than all the others.

This man was dangerous. He was bigger than she expected. He had a hard edge showing even through the exhaustion. His jaw was squared denoting stubbornness.

The tingling sense of awareness that shivered across her skin when he looked at her warned as nothing else could. He could also be very dangerous to her peace of mind. There was something blatantly masculine about him despite his temporary injured state. A kind of arrogant, don't-give-a-hoot attitude that appealed to women the world over.

She'd love to have that attention turned on her.

No, she wouldn't. He was light years out of her league.

Shifting her gaze to the sleeping baby, she refused to allow herself to even imagine there could be any sort of relationship between her and her new employer beside the boss-nanny one.

She was so not interested in men with children! No matter how gorgeous they looked or how feminine they made her feel. They were forever off-limits!

The heavy, humid air seemed to vaporize and she had

trouble drawing a breath. She wondered suddenly how she could have agreed to a summer job without knowing more about the man with whom she would be working. Had she lost all common sense?

Or had the lure of a summer in New Orleans been too much to resist?

There was something definitely exciting about the way he looked at her. And the way that look made her feel. Her heart skipped a beat then settled in at double-time.

Jenny licked her lips as heat swirled around her. She dragged in another ragged breath. This had to stop. She was here for a job, not to conjure up some fantasy with a stranger. An injured stranger for whom any interest in the opposite gender was certainly the farthest thing from his mind.

The right leg of the jeans he wore had been cut away to accommodate the cast. The left leg snugly displayed his muscular strength. His white shirt, opened at the throat, revealed the strong column of his neck, the breadth of his shoulders. Even sitting on the sofa, obviously battered and bruised, he looked stronger and more exciting than any man she'd ever known. The air seemed to shimmer with his masculinity.

Wow, she'd be cooped up with him all summer? Anticipation and apprehension mixed.

Her gaze darting over him, Jenny noticed the pain lines bracketing his mouth, the tight look on his face. He was in obvious discomfort. She felt like an idiot for letting her mind wander. The new nanny was probably the last thing on his mind.

"Do you need anything?" she asked, feeling she needed to do something to earn her keep.

"A glass of water would be great." He reached into his shirt pocket and pulled out a small packet of pills. "I held off taking these so I'd stay awake for the baby. But I sure wouldn't mind a couple now."

She hurried into the kitchen, glad for something to do beside stare at the man. Running water into a glass, she took a deep breath before returning. She almost laughed at her foolishness. The man was injured and not a bit interested in anything but a good night's sleep. And in someone to watch his daughter.

She handed him the glass, startled at the spark that jumped between them when his fingertips brushed against hers. He took hold of the glass, she pulled back. The tingle of his touch lingered.

Almost forcing herself to move away, Jenny crossed to the baby. She was much smaller than Jenny had expected. Flicking a glance at Jared, she knelt near the carrier, fussing needlessly with the light blanket. She'd been hired by Jared's sister to watch this baby during the time it took Jared to recover from his injuries. She needed to demonstrate she was capable of doing that job before he questioned her abilities.

Jenny loved babies. Always had. One day she hoped she'd have a house full of her own. Until then, she satisfied her interest and delight in children by teaching elementary school.

Sighing quietly, she tried to focus her attention on the child and ignore the awareness that seemed to center around the man on the sofa.

Easier said than done.

Had she let her joy at obtaining a coveted job in New Orleans, at the exact time she wanted to escape Whitney, blind her to reality? Anything that looked too good to be true probably was. She knew she'd have primary care of the baby for several weeks. And cook for the father until he was ready to go it alone.

Why hadn't she given any thought to the man himself? Or the difficulties that could arise sharing close quarters? Why hadn't she given any thought to the possibility of an attraction that she was having a hard time denying?

She could be excused on the last part, she thought, never having experienced such instant attraction before. One-sided—she knew she had to watch herself. Maybe things would feel differently in the morning.

"What's her name? Your sister Patti didn't know," she added, trailing a fingertip lightly down the baby's soft cheek. She wasn't as plump as some babies Jenny knew. She had a head full of curly black hair. Were her eyes blue like her father's?

An odd fact, she thought again, that the sister hadn't known her niece's name. Didn't he communicate with his family?

If she had a family, she'd be in constant contact.

"Her name's Jamie. I hope you know how to take care of a baby, because I don't have a clue. She's asleep now, but she spent most of the trip crying."

His bafflement in dealing with the infant clearly showed in his eyes as he gazed at her.

"Oh."

Asleep in the baby carrier, Jamie slumped over to one side. Her eyes were tightly closed and her cheeks were almost drawn, not plump and rosy like the babies Jenny used to help with. Her heart went out to the little girl, she longed to pick her up and cuddle her—but Jamie obviously needed the rest. She looked exhausted. Jenny didn't want to chance waking her.

"I imagine the trip was hard for her. I don't think babies can adjust their ear pressure easily when flying," she said.

"I'm not sure it was just the flight. I got out of the hospital a day ago, and she pretty much cried the entire time I was making arrangements for the trip," he said wryly. "I guess I don't have the paternal touch."

Jenny wanted to ask if he'd held her and rocked her, but he looked in too much need of care himself. Hadn't there been anyone else to watch over her? To assist him on the long journey back to the states?

What had happened to the baby's mother? Patti said only that the woman was dead. It hadn't mattered at the time, but now curiosity reared up. She wanted to learn all she could about this precious baby.

"If you want to go on up to bed, I'll take care of her from now on," Jenny said softly. She couldn't wait to hold her, rock her, cuddle with her.

Jared shook his head. "I can't make another flight of stairs tonight. I'll just bunk down here." He leaned his head back and closed his eyes. "I expect the pills will kick in soon and I'll be out like a light. I sure hope so."

A wave of sympathy washed through Jenny. He'd made the entire journey without pain medication when he so clearly needed it. The least she could do was make sure he didn't have to worry now. She'd watch Jamie and give him the respite he needed.

"I'll take her upstairs with me, then," she said.

Jenny knew children, had dealt with babies galore while growing up. Wasn't that the primary reason Patti had offered her the job? Jenny also suspected Patti had heard about Jenny's broken engagement and knew this job would provide a welcomed alternative to remaining in Whitney for the summer. As a means to escape the awkwardness and gossip among their fellow teachers, a few weeks in New Orleans couldn't be beat.

While people agreed to marry and then broke up all the time, it felt awkward when she was one of the parties involved.

"How old is Jamie? Isn't she young to be traveling so far?" She turned to look at Jared.

"She's two months, small for her age, I guess." His eyes were still closed. He looked exhausted.

Jenny knew from Patti that he'd been stationed at an American oil field in the Middle East. But that area covered a lot of countries. Finding herself consumed with curiosity about her new employer as well as the baby, she longed to question him, but hesitated, unsure how much he'd want to reveal. Or how much he would think she needed to know.

She was only the temporary summer nanny for his daughter.

Heat stole into her cheeks. Once again she was forgetting the baby. She was certain Jared Montgomery would no more be interested in her than any of the boys had at the J. P. Whitney Home for Children when she'd been a teenager.

But it didn't stop the sudden wish that she was more worldly, that she had a way with men that was legendary. That she could laugh and flirt with the best of them—enticing them outrageously. And be able to ignore the clamoring of her own senses.

Sighing softly, she knew she'd be foolish to long for attention from this man. He was far too injured right now to be interested in anyone. And wasn't he recovering from the recent loss of the baby's mother? Mourning one woman would definitely put him off getting involved with another.

Despite her being blond with a nice figure, men just didn't fall over themselves to ask her out. She was a bit shy and dressed conservatively—she knew she wasn't what men dreamed about. Even Tad had rarely pushed for anything more than a chaste kiss goodnight and he had purported to want to marry her!

The cab driver stomped back up the stairs, pushed open the door, his arms and hands loaded with bags and suitcases and a utilitarian diaper bag. Dumping them on the floor with a clatter, he looked chagrined when the baby jerked and awoke.

"Sorry, they slipped," he said.

Soft fretful cries began to fill the room.

Jared peeled several dollars from his wallet and held them out for the cab driver. "Thanks for bringing up the bags and for the extra help."

"Sure thing." The driver quickly pocketed the money and headed for the door. In seconds it closed behind him. Only the cries of the baby remained.

Jenny needed no prompting. She hated to hear babies cry. Reaching down to unfasten the carrier straps, she lifted the infant into her arms. The child weighed practically nothing. Light and petite, notwithstanding, she could cry with the best of them. Her wails almost hurt Jenny's ears.

"I'd hoped she'd sleep through the night. She cried enough on the plane to be exhausted. Do you think she's hungry? Or maybe just startled awake by the noise." Jared rubbed his eyes with one hand, then looked at the baby. Reaching for his crutches, he sat up.

"Shh, shh, shh," Jenny crooned to her, cuddling her close to her breast. "There, there, pumpkin, everything will be all right. Did that loud noise wake you up?" She rocked back and forth, trying to comfort the baby.

"She might be hungry, she seems to eat all the time. There's some formula in that blue bag on the right. Diapers are in there, too." Jared sat on the edge of the sofa, hands already on the crutches.

Jenny looked over her shoulder. Jared swayed as he rose.

"Stay there. I'll take care of Jamie. If she hasn't eaten in a while, she probably is hungry. I'll fix her a bottle and take her upstairs. We'll be fine. You take care of yourself—get some rest."

Jared nodded at her words, but his eyes continued to watch her as if to make sure she was taking proper care of the baby.

"I didn't know babies weren't good travelers. The flight attendant on the plane to New Orleans from New York took her a lot and walked around with her."

"It's a big change to fly for so long. She'll be fine soon." Jenny rummaged around in the bag containing bottles and formula. In only a moment she had what she wanted and headed for the kitchen.

It was awkward to prepare the bottle one-handed, but she tried to soothe the baby as she worked. When the bottle was ready, Jamie latched onto it as if she were starving.

Jenny carried her back to the living room. Jared was again leaning back against the cushions, his eyes closed.

"Good night," Jenny said, grabbing the diaper bag. She would rather stay and get to know Jared, but he looked exhausted. Rest would be good for both him and the baby.

"Ummm," he mumbled, already nine-tenths asleep.

After she'd seen to the baby, she'd come back downstairs to make sure he was lying down. Maybe even bring a light blanket in case it cooled off during the night. But first, she needed to get the baby settled.

Jared listened as Jenny crooned to the baby. The sound of her footsteps faded as she climbed the stairs to the second floor of the apartment. Had his sister lost her marbles? What had she been thinking, sending a beautiful blonde to help a man who had been stationed in the Middle East for several years?

Beautiful and young. And obviously crazy about kids.

He suspected what Patti had been thinking. Matchmaking again, unless he missed his guess.

Maybe one day his sister would get it in her head that he had no interest in marriage again or a family! Andrea had cured him of that. Andrea and his own father.

Jenny could stay until he'd found a permanent solution to the situation with Jamie, but only as a nanny for the baby. He'd remain immune to her appeal.

Patti was happily married to her high school sweetheart and couldn't understand her older brother's aversion to that institution.

Her efforts at getting him married again would fail as her previous ones had. He was returning to the Middle East as soon as his ankle healed. After the explosion, the whole oil field was suspect and new tests were needed to see if other unexpected pockets of gas were hidden. Not that the company would wait for his return to commence the cleanup. But once he was fit, there'd still be plenty to do to get the wells producing again.

He adjusted one cushion as a pillow and lay down. Just before sleep claimed him, he almost smiled. He'd resist temptation but enjoy the process. It could take a while to find a home for Jamie. In the meantime, he had a beautiful woman sharing his apartment.

And there wasn't anything he could do about it.

Jenny sat on the edge of a bed, watching Jamie as the baby drank ravenously from the bottle. Why had Jared insisted on coming to New Orleans and hiring a stranger to take care of his child when he had family just a few hours away who would love to help out?

And why didn't his family know more about the baby and what had happened to her mother?

Jenny had a hundred questions—including ones about that odd attraction that had exploded inside her whenever she looked at Jared Montgomery.

Feeling foolish, she restated her resolve—she would never again get involved with a man who had a child. After the way she'd fallen for Tad, she'd learned her lesson. She'd thought his love words had been real because he cared for her, and not simply to coax her into a marriage to watch his two rapscallion boys. She had loved those little boys, but loved the father more.

Until her love had been betrayed.

It was a hard lesson--but one learned well.

Once she'd discovered the truth, she vowed to realize her dream of a perfect family only with a man who did not come to the marriage with any baggage from a previous relationship-- who only wanted a wife to take on his family.

She wanted to start her family from scratch.

And to know she was loved for herself.

"Even if your daddy is a heartthrob," she whispered to the baby as Jamie greedily sucked on the nipple. "He's definitely off-limits! What happened to your mommy, little one?"

Jenny remembered the bare-bones explanation that Jared's sister had given. The baby was the result of an affair in the Arabian country where Jared was working. The mother had died. One of the oil rigs had exploded, killing several workers and injuring a score more, including her brother. He had no one to take care of the baby. He was being rotated home until he recovered enough from his injuries to return to work. And, it was assumed, to find someone permanent to take care of his child.

Jenny had been delighted to take on the assignment—watch the baby for a few weeks during the summer until a permanent arrangement was made. The timing had been ideal, starting just a few days after school ended for the term. To find a job with room and board thrown in—right in the heart of the French Quarter—seemed like a dream.

But now Jenny wondered if she should have questioned the circumstances a bit more. Learned more about what was expected.

And learned a lot more about Jared Montgomery.

Chapter Two

Jenny found Jared totally fascinating the few minutes they'd spent together. She'd definitely not expected that. Wary around men after discovering Tad's perfidy, she'd planned a carefree summer— not an instant wild attraction!

Tomorrow, she'd reassess the situation. She was probably reacting to the ambiance of the romantic French Quarter. He was a man who needed help with his child. She could provide it while his injuries healed.

And any fascination she felt could and would be ruthlessly eliminated!

She'd make this the ideal job. By fall, all gossip about her broken engagement to Tad would have faded and she could return to school ready for a new school year.

In the morning, she'd fix Jared's breakfast and discuss his expectations for Jamie. Beyond that, they'd go their separate ways.

Slowly she shook her head. She couldn't envision sharing the apartment for a few weeks with the man without also longing for things that would never be. One look from his blue eyes and she'd forget what she was supposed to be doing.

Not that he'd look at her in any light but that of a nanny. Granted she'd done more than her share of watching babies as she'd grown up in the Home for Children, now she was an elementary school teacher, not some exciting, worldly temptress.

She looked at the baby. "It's not that I don't want to watch you, pumpkin, but I'm not real sure about what to expect from your daddy. I sure didn't anticipate this unsettling reaction tonight!"

Jamie chewed on the rubber nipple, her dark eyes fixed on Jenny's face.

"Finished eating, sweetie?" Jenny asked, gently pulling the bottle away and placing the baby upright against her shoulder. Gently she rubbed her back, wishing she had a rocking chair.

There had been six or seven at the Home. She'd loved to sit in a big old chair and rock the babies. The lazy fan in the high ceiling had stirred the hot air, but never completely cooled the room. It hadn't mattered. In those days, Jenny had never lived in an air-conditioned home. A child didn't miss what she'd never known. The South was hot and humid and that was just the way it was.

In the distance, thunder rumbled. The curtains flanking the tall windows shifted in the growing strength of the breeze. Cool air wafted into the high-ceilinged room. Somehow it seemed wrong to use air-conditioning so close to the river. Maybe during the heat of the day, but in the evenings Jenny hoped she could keep the windows open and enjoy the sounds and smells of the famous French Quarter.

"Feels good, doesn't it, Jamie? You can sleep well tonight, babykins, it won't be too hot."

Jenny hummed to the baby as she patted her back. She wondered if Jared was already asleep. She'd opened the French doors leading to the balcony when she first arrived. Surely he was enjoying the breeze as well. It could grow cooler during the night. Maybe she should run downstairs to check to see if he needed something.

"Right."

Heat blossomed again and she frowned. Her fair skin was the bane of her existence. Even when she tried to keep a poker face, a blush of embarrassment often tinted her cheeks, announcing to the world what she'd rather keep hidden.

Jenny wasn't sure what arrangements Jared planned to make concerning Jamie. He probably needed to find a live-in housekeeper to watch the baby while he went to work. How long could that take? Just a few days or maybe a couple of weeks at the most.

But until then, she'd escaped from Whitney. For the moment, that was enough.

With room and board included in this assignment in addition to pay, if it ended before summer did, she might have enough to stay longer in New Orleans and play tourist. She wasn't going to let one set back stop her from enjoying life.

"Tad." She said the name aloud, and then slowly smiled.

For the first time in the two months since she'd discovered he meant only to marry her to obtain a mother for his sons, his name didn't bring an ache to her heart.

She'd been devastated when she'd overheard his comments to a friend at a spring barbecue they'd attended together. Did the entire town know he thought she'd make a great mother for his sons? Even when she'd confronted him he'd only shrugged. They were good together, he said. She was excellent with the boys. Everyone won, he'd said.

What about making a great wife for him? That thought had apparently never crossed his mind.

Maybe the love she thought she felt for Tad had been fostered by her own ardent yearning for a family. Was she as guilty as Tad of planing to marry without true and lasting love? Wishing for a husband, any husband, and those darling boys to complete her life had she pretended everything was the way she wanted?

She remembered the doubts she'd tried so hard to ignore. Once faced with the fact Tad didn't love her, she'd instantly ended their engagement.

The offer of a job for the summer in New Orleans a week ago had freed her from the embarrassment she felt when others commiserated with her on the breakup.

Now that she was here, Jenny was pleased to discover she felt no twinge of regret at the ending of their engagement. She'd made the right decision.

"Remember that, babykins. Don't go marrying someone just to complete a family. God has someone out there for you and me. Special, just for us. Someone who will love us for ourselves and want to build a family together. A perfect family, where we'll all love each other and share similar interests and activities. Hold out for that yourself, pumpkin. Anything less won't make you happy."

Jamie's head wobbled on her short neck, then crashed against Jenny's shoulder.

"Oh, honey, don't hurt yourself." Jenny laid the baby on her lap, and held her hands, playing patty-cake for a few minutes. "I'm tired, how about you?"

She made a bed of sorts for Jamie, using one of the large drawers from the old dresser placed on the floor and pillows from the bed she planned to use. Laying the baby in the makeshift crib, she wondered why Jared hadn't sent ahead to have baby furniture waiting.

Or gone home to his family in Whitney. That sparked her curiosity even more.

His mother could have watched the baby and taken care of him while he recuperated. Why hire a stranger? Why insist on staying in New Orleans? His apartment wasn't convenient for a man with mobility problems. And from what she'd learned from Mrs. Giraux after meeting the woman that afternoon, Jared didn't have a lot of close friends to rally around. He was gone more than he was home.

Maybe he wasn't thinking clearly as a result of the explosion.

Time enough in the morning to find out what she needed to know. She'd counted on a summer in New Orleans. Now she had to make sure she could stay and remain immune to that hunk of a daddy.

Leaving the door ajar, she left the bedroom. She'd found a sparse linen closet when exploring the apartment upon her arrival. She withdrew a light summer blanket and stole quietly down the stairs. The lights were still on. Jared was fast asleep.

She unlaced his shoe and pulled it off, doing her best not to disturb him. She suspected the pain pills had knocked him out but she didn't want to take the chance. It was beginning to cool down now with the breeze blowing in from the square. She draped the light blanket over him, studying him as he slept

She winced as she realized how hard his head must have been hit to produce such bruises. Wondered if there were other bruises on his body—which she'd never know, she warned herself.

Quickly switching off the lights, one by one, she hurried back up the stairs. She had no business fantasizing about her new employer. This had to stop.

Slipping beneath the cool sheets a few minutes later, she considered that she had never felt that kind of intensity around Tad, like she wanted to reach out and wrap her arms around the man, mold her body against his and never let go.

Good grief, was she going crazy? Was the air in New Orleans saturated with romance so foolish thoughts abounded?

Turning to her side, Jenny tried to think of something else. The curtains moved in the air as a breeze from the river skipped across the old square. The thunder faded. The storm would bypass New Orleans, she thought sleepily. It was too bad, they could use its cooling relief.

Slowly Jenny drifted to sleep, dreaming of a dark- haired man who brought child after child to her to watch. She couldn't say no, not when he smiled.

Chapter Three

The fragrance of freshly brewed coffee filled the room. Jared moved slowly, his eyes opening. When he recognized his apartment, realized he was home, satisfaction filled him. He'd shower and dress, then head for the Café du Monde for some hot beignets and café au lait. It was the best part of returning home. His first-morning-back ritual.

When he went to get up, his stiff muscles protested. He closed his eyes, instantly his memory returned in full force. The explosion, the days in the hospital.

The news about Jim. His best friend since the second grade was dead. He still had trouble believing it. The man who had been closer than a brother to him was gone.

As was Sohany. That had been another shock.

And he was left with a two-month-old infant!

Rubbing his eyes with one hand, he opened them and stared at the ceiling. They'd made it home. Patti had hired someone to watch the baby until he could find a permanent solution. The sooner he found a home for Jamie, the sooner she could start her new life and he'd have fulfilled his obligation to his friend.

But first, he had to get up.

And face Jenny Stratford.

He knew he'd never told his sister about his weakness for blondes. Or that he liked his women tall and shapely. For a moment he let the memories from last night replay in his mind. Jenny had looked far too young to be responsible for an infant was his first thought when he'd seen her beneath the weak hallway light.

He revised that opinion once he observed her dealing with Jamie.

Her silky, champagne-colored hair, large blue eyes, and pale pink cheeks made a man thankful that he called the States home. Her straight hair looked to be the kind that rarely held a curl, but enticed a man to touch, to thread through his fingers, to savor the softness against his skin. He could almost feel those silky strands. Fisting his hands, he shook his head to clear the images that danced before him.

He'd been too long in the Middle East. Jenny was a looker—no denying that. But not for him. He was not in line for any kind of long-term relationship. He'd seen what such an arrangement could do—destroy a man's ambitions and plans He wanted no part of it again. He'd sworn off marriage.

He had tried it with Andrea. And had chafed at the restrictions, felt imprisoned with her demands and her dreams once they'd started their life together. She'd known of his ambitions as long as she'd known him. But she had thought they'd change once married.

She'd had a different agenda. And her goals hadn't been his.

He wished he'd realized that before they married. But in all the years they dated, and made plans, she'd never voiced her true beliefs until after the ring was on her finger.

It had taken two years before he finally admitted defeat

and severed the relationship. Two years of disillusionment and disappointment on both sides.

At least he'd learned from the experience. Had learned how to avoid a future mistake.

He had his future mapped out now. He was footloose and free with no woman trying to force his life to her standards. He wouldn't become trapped in the kind of life his father still bemoaned. Jared wasn't sure it made him smarter than his old man, but he sure took the lesson to heart .

Since his divorce, he'd never dated any one woman more than two or three times.

Slowly he sat, sliding his legs over the edge of the sofa. Time to get moving. The sooner he took care of the baby's future, the sooner he could send pretty Jenny Stratford back to Whitney before he did something foolish. Like give in to the shimmering urge to kiss her that had flooded him when he'd stood on those stairs last night and let his gaze drift up her long legs.

Like imagining wrapping the strands of that silky hair around his hands to pull her closer. Like feeling those pink lips against his.

Stifling a groan, he drew the crutches closer and stood up. Once he was mobile, he'd hunt up some old girlfriend and do the town. Wincing as he stood, he wondered how long it would be before he became fully mobile again.

Jenny heard the thump of crutches on the stairs and sat up. Time to get dressed and start earning her keep.

The baby had wakened just before dawn. Jenny had crept down the stairs and prepared a bottle for her, noticing at the time that Jared still slept soundly.

Feeding Jamie and changing her had put her right back to sleep. Unable to use the living room, Jenny had crawled back into bed as well. Now she could get up.

Jenny glanced at Jamie's small form beneath the baby blanket. The dim morning light gave the illusion of quiet, though the sounds from the square began to filter in through the open window. Tiny and fragile, Jamie slept deeply, her chest rising and falling as she breathed.

Was it her imagination or did she already look healthier?

"Poor baby," Jenny murmured, wondering how long it would take for good food to fill her out and plump her up like most babies.

"What happened to your mommy, babykins?" she asked softly, curiosity raging.

Obviously Jared wasn't used to being around a baby. He'd seemed totally helpless dealing with his daughter last night. Was he the kind of man who thought raising children was women's work?

Maybe.

Yet he'd watched her with the baby like a hawk as if to insure she didn't make a mistake with Jamie. She wouldn't want to run afoul of him.

The soft thudding on the stairs went on for several minutes. It must be extremely frustrating for him—to be so limited by his injuries. She bet normally he was active and full of energy. The image that danced before her eyes had her throwing back the covers and jumping from the bed.

She dressed quickly. When she heard the shower, she lifted the makeshift crib and carried it awkwardly down the stairs and set it in a dim corner of the living room. Until she got a baby monitor, she didn't want to leave Jamie alone.

The sun had already begun warming the day. The aroma of freshly brewed coffee drifted in through the open French doors. Her mouth watered. Wandering out onto the balcony, she gazed at the setting and waited for Jared to come back downstairs.

When she heard him sometime later, she went back into the living room. "Good morning," she said brightly as he reached the bottom step.

"Is she still sleeping?" he asked, moving quietly across the room on the crutches to peer down at Jamie in her makeshift bed.

"She woke earlier and as soon as I fed her, she went right back to sleep. I don't know her schedule, so I don't know if she'll stay asleep for long, or wake up soon."

Jared shrugged. "I don't know either."

Jenny looked at him, puzzled. The man could take a bit more interest in his daughter. Granted, he'd been in the hospital for the last several weeks, but he must have observed her routine before that.

He caught her look.

"I was in the hospital until a couple of days ago. Her aunt was watching her. When she couldn't do it anymore, I checked out and headed for home."

"You'll get used to her routine soon."

"I've never been around babies much," he said slowly, looking at the little one asleep. "She's tiny, isn't she?"

"They grow fast. I'll fix a bottle and you can feed her when she wakes up if you wish," she offered.

"She'll feel more comfortable with a woman, I think," he said, turning to head toward the kitchen. Jenny followed him to the doorway.

"I want to take a quick shower," she said. "I'm sure she'll stay asleep for a while. Can I get you anything first?"

He shook his head. "Take your shower and then you can get us some breakfast. If that's okay with you?"

He looked at her, raising one eyebrow.

She nodded and felt the flush of heat wash into her cheeks. It should be easy to resist, she'd just met the man a few hours ago.

She sought for something to say, hoping he never realized the effect his presence had on her.

"Is the baby furniture arriving today?"

Jared shrugged. "We can get a crib or something to tide us over."

"Tide us over? What does that mean?"

"Didn't Patti tell you the job was temporary, until other arrangements could be made?" Jared asked. He leaned against the counter, folding his arms across his chest. The crutches rested beside him.

"Yes." Jenny was hard put to keep her eyes locked onto his. They had a tendency to want to trail down his body.

She'd done her share of studying good-looking men from a distance, but never felt the compelling desire to catalogue every aspect before. From the individual features of his face to the fact he seemed to epitomize masculinity, she wished she could stare at him all day. She swallowed and tried to ignore her clamoring senses.

"It shouldn't take long to find a family for Jamie. It seems to me that I've heard for years about the shortage of adoptable children. She's just an infant, prime age for adoption," Jared said slowly.

"Adoption? You're going to put Jamie up for adoption?" Jenny couldn't believe her ears. "Your own daughter!"

All the anguish and despair she'd felt as an orphan rose up and threatened to choke her. How many times had she dreamed of discovering a long-lost relative, someone with whom she could have lived, grown up with, made memories and started traditions with? Someone to tell her about her parents, about her family, long gone now.

The years had not extinguished that need.

And now a child's father was planning to give her up for adoption? Not for financial reasons, or health reasons, or family reasons. Not for any good reason that she could see. What kind of man was he?

"My name may be on the birth certificate, but Jamie's not mine," he said.

Jenny stared at him in stunned silence. Jamie wasn't his? But hadn't Patti said her brother needed someone to watch his child?

"I don't understand," she said slowly. "Whose child is she? How did your name get on the birth certificate if she's not yours?"

"It's a long story. Take your shower, then you can go out and get us some breakfast," Jared said, as he glanced at an empty cupboard. He frowned as he looked back at Jenny. "You'll have to go shopping today. There's nothing to eat."

"What do you want for breakfast?" Jenny asked, backing toward the door, wanting to shower, dress, pick up breakfast in record time to get back to the apartment as soon as she could to hear that long story. His comments whetted her curiosity.

"When did you get to New Orleans?" he asked, tilting his head, a slight smile playing around his lips.

"About four o'clock yesterday afternoon," she replied, bewitched by that half smile.

"Beignets and coffee from the Café du Monde," he said firmly. "It's the only way to celebrate your first morning in the Crescent City."

Jenny nodded. That did sound like a great tradition. At least they agreed on one thing.

"I'll hurry," she said.

Chapter Four

The beignets were still warm and heavily dusted with powdered sugar. The café au lait's fragrance delighted her senses. The two of them sat at the small table on the balcony. Jackson Square was coming alive and the heat was beginning to be felt, but it was almost surreal to be eating the delicious New Orleans' specialty.

Jenny sipped slowly, savoring the delicious hint of chicory in the coffee. She glanced into the living room at the baby. Still asleep. Bless her heart, she must have been exhausted after her recent journey.

"Tell me something about yourself, Jenny Stratford," Jared said as he reached into the white bag and withdrew two more beignets. Powdered sugar spilled on the table.

"I'd rather hear about Jamie," she said.

"That story will keep a little longer. I want to hear about you first. Where're you from? How did my sister know to hire you? Why did you take the job? It's not going to last for long."

Jenny took a deep breath, biting back a sharp retort. Her curiosity was raging and he wanted to talk about her. She knew all about herself.

"I was born in Whitney, grew up there and then returned after college. I teach in the primary school where your sister works. I wanted a summer job and when Patti offered this I said yes."

"Succinct," he murmured.

She shifted slightly in her chair, uncomfortably aware of the intensity of his regard and the heart- pounding reaction she seemed to experience in his proximity. She needed to get a hold of her emotions, get them under control. Just because he was drop-dead gorgeous was no reason to lose her head.

Focus on his cynicism, that should dampen any attraction, she thought desperately.

He was her employer—for the time being at least. And even if he wasn't, there was no future in getting interested in the man. He probably ate inexperienced women like her for breakfast.

She glanced at the ring of white powder surrounding his mouth. When, she amended, he wasn't eating beignets for breakfast.

She had the almost overwhelming urge to brush that powdered sugar from around his lips. Heat seeped through her and she looked away, hoping frantically that he couldn't read minds.

"Do your folks still live in Whitney? Are they friends with mine?" he asked.

"My parents are dead," she replied. "When Patti heard I might wish to leave Whitney for the summer, she approached me about this job."

"Leave?"

"Find somewhere else to spend the summer vacation," she said vaguely.

"As in escape?"

She frowned, heat creeping into her cheeks again. He

couldn't read minds!

"I just wanted to—"

"Escape from what?" Jared asked, putting down his half-eaten beignet and studying her, obviously intrigued.

"I've always thought it would be great to live in New Orleans. When Patti told me the job would be here, I jumped at it. That hardly constitutes an escape."

"Coming here to work for a few weeks still gets you out of Whitney. If that's your home and where you work, why did you want to leave?"

She frowned at his tenacity. "I wanted to avoid an awkward situation, all right?"

She studied the powdered sugar on the table, tracing random patterns with her fingertip. Beignets were delicious, but sure messy.

"What awkward situation?"

She gave him an exasperated look. She wouldn't be leaving the situation behind if she had to continually explain it to all and sundry.

"What does it matter?"

"Just curious."

"Well, I'm curious about Jamie. You say she's not yours, but your name is on her birth certificate. Odd," Jenny said slowly, reaching for another beignet. Could someone become addicted to the delicious French pastry after one serving?

Jared leaned back in his chair. Seated, his broken ankle was hidden. But in the bright daylight Jenny saw the bruises that lingered as an after effect of the explosion. She shivered suddenly, aware that this man could have lost his life in the accident. Oil rigs and danger seemed to go together. How did a man choose that line of work as a profession?

His hair was in disarray, as if he'd dragged his fingers through it. She longed to brush it into some order. His blue chambray shirt outlined his shoulders, tapered to the trim waistband of the ubiquitous jeans. Jenny took the opportunity to study the man when he talked.

She was enthralled with him, almost to the exclusion of anything else.

Why? What was it that made him seem larger than life? The scars from his accident? His size? Or some special aura that made him seem so much more masculine than the men she normally associated with? So much more tempting.

Was it the travel, the patina of foreign places, an exotic profession?

Or was she simply on the rebound from Tad? Seeing fascination where none existed?

Jenny didn't want to admit it, even to herself, but she wondered if something was lacking within her that no man had found her suitable for a mate. She thought Tad had, but it had only proved to be expedient for him to find a wife. And who better to manage his six- and seven-year-old sons than a primary school teacher?

She couldn't believe she'd thought he loved her.

She was wiser now.

"You said it was a long story, we have time now." She refused to be put off any longer.

"It's a variation on an old, tired theme. Jim Draydon was a friend of mine." Jared hesitated a long moment. "A good friend. We grew up together, attended the same university. Even got our jobs with the same company. We worked together for years, first in several fields in the Sahara then in Kuwait. This last assignment in the U.A.E. was just one in a long string," Jared said.

He had devoured his share of the beignets as if starving. Now tilted back in his chair, he cradled a cup of coffee against his chest. His eyes gazed out toward the cathedral but she knew he was seeing all the way to the Middle East.

"This tour, however, he fell in love with a local woman, Sohany Ibenetz. I mean he really fell hard. Before I knew it, they were living together."

His blue eyes flashed to her and he frowned.

Jenny kept her face passive. It was not her place to pass judgement—but she could tell Jared hadn't approved.

"Then Sohany became pregnant," he said.

"So did your friend marry her?" she asked when he paused.

"A bit hard to do, Jim was already married—had been for years. Margaret and he have three kids, two boys and a girl."

"Oh, no." Jenny's eyes widened at the revelation. She glanced into the living room. Poor child—what a legacy.

"So you put your name down on the birth certificate to help your friend?" she asked turning back to Jared.

"No. Sohany had the baby. Jim was frantic about what he would tell his wife, his other kids. He didn't want to let Sohany down, nor his new baby, but he had obligations and responsibilities in the States, too."

"Seems to me he should have remembered those a bit earlier," Jenny said tartly.

The muscles in his cheeks clenched. He was angry—at his friend? Or at her for her comment? Or at fate for landing him in this situation?

"So what did he do? How did your friend convince you to take charge of a two-month-old infant? And what of Jamie's mother? Is she coming to join you soon?" Jenny asked when the silence stretched out longer than her patience.

"In the end, there was no decision to be made. Jim was killed in that explosion three weeks ago. He'd once asked me to make sure Sohany and the baby were taken care of if he couldn't be there. At the time I thought he meant if he returned to Margaret and ended his relationship with Sohany. I agreed. But he died— leaving the whole mess in my lap."

"Where is Sohany now?" Jenny asked gently, sympathizing with the grief at his friend's death.

"She died last week of pneumonia."

Jenny stared at him, an odd little prickle playing on the nape of her neck. "My mother died of pneumonia," she murmured. So she and little Jamie had something in common. Both were orphans, both their mothers had died from pneumonia. How odd.

"That was the official version. I think she just couldn't bear to hang around after Jim was killed. She'd been ailing since the birth. She came to see me in the hospital two days after Jim's death and asked if she could count on me to watch out for Jamie. Jim had told her he had asked me."

Jared's expression gave nothing away. Jenny knew he must still be grieving for his friend.

"I told Sohany I'd do all I could. She coughed the entire visit. I didn't realize she was so sick. If anything happened to her, it would simplify things if I was listed as Jamie's father, she said. I agreed—I think. I was so doped up on narcotics for the pain, I probably would have agreed to sign over my pension."

"So your name's on the birth certificate. That must have made it a lot easier for you to bring her home."

"That and the fact the Arabs were delighted to have a problem solved so easily. No one even questioned me."

"And your friend's wife? Are you planning to tell her about the child?"

Jared shook his head. Taking a last swallow from his cup, he slammed it down on the table. "No. I considered it. But Jim's parents are dead. He has no other family besides Margaret and his children. Why sully their memories of him? Learning about his affair would only bring them heartache. And I sure can't see Margaret raising Jamie, so what's the point in their knowing?"

Jenny was oddly touched that Jared felt so strongly about protecting his friend's memory, and was taking responsibility for his friend's child. Maybe there was something to genuinely admire about this man besides how he looked or made her feel.

"Taking on a baby is a big responsibility for anyone," Jenny said softly.

"Especially if a baby is the result of your husband's infidelity. I can't imagine any woman who would cheerfully take that on."

"I guess not. Thank the Lord, Jamie has you," she said.

"Don't go getting all sentimental. I'm in no position to take care of a baby. I haven't been around babies much. My job takes me all over the world—and in places I wouldn't take an adult, much less an infant. I'll take steps to find her a good home, a two-parent home, where they want a child and can give her all she needs in life."

"Couldn't you raise her yourself?" Jenny asked. "I mean, I know you're single, but you could hire a live- in nanny, more permanent than I'll be, someone to watch her and keep house for you."

"I considered that, but it won't work. I travel extensively, am rarely in the States—and then it's not for more than a month at a time. What if the housekeeper quits, or gets sick, or something? How would I hire someone else from an oil field somewhere in the Middle East?"

"You have family around who could help in an emergency," she pointed out.

"There's only so much they could do. They don't live here. Problems that might arise in New Orleans would be difficult for them to deal with from Whitney."

"So relocate to Whitney," she suggested, wondering again why he kept a place in New Orleans if he was so rarely home.

"That is definitely not an option."

She blinked at his adamant tone. Questions again rose, but she ignored her curiosity. There had to be a solution to this situation that would enable Jamie to stay in close contact with her father's friend.

"You could always get married," she said softly, for the first time fully understanding Tad's need for a wife—for someone to share the burden of caring for his children with him. Maybe she'd judged him too harshly. There were many reasons for a marriage. She wanted love to be the foremost for hers, but that didn't mean everyone felt the same way.

Of course, most people came from a stable, loving family background. With that in their lives, a more businesslike approach to marriage might be acceptable. But when one was an orphan, had been for more than two decades, love was most important. That and a sense of belonging, of being wanted, and valued and loved for herself alone.

"No way." His tone firmly closed that avenue of discussion.

Why was he so adamant against marriage? Another question to add to the growing number in her mind. Would she ever find a chance to ask them?

Her heart ached for the little orphan in the next room. Would it be truly better for Jamie if Jared found a family to give her to? Jenny wasn't convinced. Had he considered the baby's point of view? The questions she'd have in the future?

"You knew her mother and father. As she's growing up you could give her a sense of her own history, her family background. That's very precious," she said.

He looked at her sharply. "How long have your parents been dead?"

"My father died before I was born, my mother when I was four. I barely remember anything about her. There's no one who knew them. Apparently they moved to Whitney just before my father died. I don't know where they came from, if there were any other relatives. I have no family history. That's why I know how important it is. Think of Jamie before rashly altering her life."

"So who raised you?" he asked.

"I grew up in the J. P. Whitney Home for Children."

"The orphanage in Whitney?"

She nodded.

"I didn't know."

"It's a nice place. Well-run and the staff's very loving and kind," she defended. "It's the only home I can remember."

"You were never adopted?"

She shook her head, smiling ruefully. "I wasn't the most docile of children. And not being very pretty, most people—"

"Not pretty? Have you looked in the mirror lately?" he interrupted, his eyes narrowed as he stared at her.

Surprised delight washed through her at his unexpected interruption. He thought she was pretty? She was speechless.

Even Tad had never called her pretty. Not that he had had much use for flowery speeches in any context.

"Okay, maybe you have a bit of a feeling for that kind of thing," he granted. "I can always visit whoever takes Jamie and tell her about her parents when she's old enough to ask questions."

"If it's an open adoption."

"What's that?"

"Often the adoption is confidential. You might not have the chance to see her after you give her up."

"I'll make sure to arrange to see her, if she wants to, when she's older. Then if she asks questions down the road, I'll be able to answer them."

"And pictures, do you have any pictures? I don't have any of my parents, of anyone in my family. I'd give anything to know what they looked like."

Jared nodded slowly. "I think I have a couple of candid shots with Jim and Sohany. I could probably get something official from Jim's file. Or ask Margaret."

"The baby had no other relatives?" Jenny asked.

"Sohany's father disowned his daughter when he discovered she was pregnant. The Arab world is very unforgiving of promiscuous behavior. She was lucky it wasn't worse. But the family thought there would be a marriage. I don't know if any knew he was already married. Her sister watched Jamie after Sohany's death. But she's engaged and with pressure from both her father and fiancé, she couldn't keep the baby."

"You're an exceptional man—to take on such a responsibility. Most of the men I know would have let the state take care of the baby or insist her natural family take her."

"Jim was my friend," Jared said simply, looking uncomfortable with her comment.

Jenny finished her coffee and wistfully wished she had more. Next time, she'd double the order. If there was a next time. She cleared her throat

"About my staying here," she began.

"I thought you'd be glad to know your stay won't be long—I'm hoping to find someone for the baby right away," he said.

"Do you have anyone in mind?"

"No, but I have a good attorney who can recommend the next step. He can either find a suitable couple or advise me as to what agencies would be the best."

"It seems a bit cold-hearted to me," she murmured, her sympathy entirely with the baby. If Jared raised Jamie, at least it would be the closest thing to her real family the baby could have.

"Well, that's the way life is sometimes." Jared pushed back his chair as if he disliked the thread of their conversation. He drew the crutches close enough to rise, then looked down at Jenny.

"As far as I can tell from this brief acquaintance, you harbor some glorified romantic notions about happy endings. The happiest ending I can give Jamie is to find her a loving home and not tie her to a nomad who never knows where he'll be next year. She'll be happy in a stable environment. That should satisfy your sensibilities."

Jenny stared at the table, listening as he made his way into the living room. He made a good point. Maybe finding the baby a loving home would be better—especially if he visited from time to time to tell Jamie about her parents. Hiring a housekeeper wouldn't be the same as providing her loving parents.

Slowly she stood and began to clear the table, wondering if she could stay until he found that family. That unexpected attraction she felt proved harder to resist as each minute ticked by. She just hoped he hadn't noticed that her emotions were in turmoil.

The awareness was compelling. She had to clench her fists at one point to keep from reaching out to brush the powdered sugar from his chin. Trace the line of his jaw. She'd kept her gaze on her food to keep from giving in to the urge to feast her eyes upon him. Holding firm on her resolve to refrain from touching him, ignoring the longings to feel the texture of his skin, to test his warmth proved harder with each passing minute.

And just when she thought she could resist him, she learned of the kindness of his sheltering his friend's first family from the knowledge of his second. That he had committed to take care of that second family, or what was left of it, the best way he knew how.

She admired him tremendously. At a time when he should be concentrating on convalescing and getting well, he had taken on an infant totally dependent upon him.

Despite everything, he'd stepped in and taken Jamie from a probable life of misery in the Middle East with no family willing to care for her, and brought her to America. Now he was doing what he thought best for his friend's child—finding her a loving home.

In the meantime, he planned to keep the baby in his apartment, and spend his own money to pay someone to watch her.

A man who took care of people no matter what the cost.

The thought hovered in her mind. What would it be like to share a life with a man like that? A man who did what he thought was right, moved ahead with plans despite his own injuries or inconveniences.

He must be grieving for his long-time friend. Did it make it that much harder to give up his friend's child? To sever the last tie he had with Jim?

Chapter Five

Jamie began to stir while Jenny was wiping the powdered sugar from the table. Hurrying across to the baby, she picked her up. Jared sat on the sofa talking on the phone, so Jenny took Jamie upstairs to change her. She gave her a quick bath, dressed her in a jumpsuit she found in the diaper bag and headed back downstairs. By this time Jamie had worked up to full-scale crying, her little face red with exertion, her fists flailing.

"Hush, honeybun. I'll have your bottle fixed in just a couple of minutes," Jenny murmured as she anticipated another juggling act, cuddling the baby while filling and heating a bottle. She should make up a couple of bottles to be prepared next time.

"Here." Jared thrust a warm bottle in her hand the minute she stepped onto the main floor.

"Thanks," Jenny said, gratefully.

She felt just a bit like she'd let him down. She was supposed to be caring for Jamie. Jared needed to care for himself, not doing her job.

"I want her to stop crying. I hate hearing her cry. Shouldn't babies be laughing and blowing bubbles?" he asked, looking at Jamie with that familiar baffled look in his eyes.

Jenny nodded. "Except when they're hungry."

She sat on the sofa, offering the bottle to the screaming infant. Instant silence. Rocking back and forth while she fed Jamie, Jenny smiled at the baby, then up at Jared.

"Nothing like a little food to put things in perspective for a baby."

He sat on the chair opposite the sofa and watched them.

"You need a rocking chair," she said after a moment. "It's great for soothing babies. You could put it on the balcony while the weather's so nice." She peeked at Jared. He continued watching her feed Jamie. Did he want a chance to hold her? Jenny wondered. Should she offer, or wait for him to ask?

He stretched out his legs and slipped his fingers into the front pockets of his jeans. He should have looked relaxed, leaning back against the cushions. But he didn't. Energy seemed to flow from him, swirl around the room, touch her.

Jenny had no problem envisioning him jumping right into action at the oil rig, even injured as he'd been. He certainly wasn't a soothing man to be around.

Exciting, though.

Despite his words about her looks at the kitchen table, he'd made no moves to show he even noticed she was a woman, much less an attractive one. It was a bit disheartening. Especially since all she could think about since last night was him.

If she could get over this fascination with Jared Montgomery, it might be possible to enjoy the job as long as he needed her. She liked babies. And, there was so much in New Orleans she wanted to explore. She needed to get her mind off the man opposite her! Of course, so far that proved easier said than done.

"Do you think it's worth buying a rocker for a few weeks at most?" Jared asked.

A few weeks? She glanced at the infant, longing to hold her even closer and protect her from all life's disappointments. Rationally she knew she shouldn't let herself become too attached to Jamie, though Jenny already felt a bond with the baby. Maybe because they were both orphans, and both their mothers had died of pneumonia. She didn't question it, but knew instinctively she wanted the very best for this child.

"I think it's worth it for however short a time she's here. A rocking chair is a great thing for a baby," she said firmly, meeting his gaze.

Jared's lips twitched, amusement shone in his eyes. "What else?"

"A crib, of course. And a stroller. I think fresh air would be good for her and I can't carry her everywhere—especially when she starts to grow," Jenny said, thinking of all the paraphernalia a baby needed.

"No high chair, bicycle, football?"

Jenny laughed softly. "Don't be silly. She can't even sit up yet. But she'll probably need some more clothes. Babies grow fast. I remember that from home."

"You call the orphanage home?"

"It was my home. And for the most part a really nice place to live. I just wish—" She stopped. It didn't matter to him what she wished. And the fervent longing for parents had faded as she'd moved into adulthood. Now she wanted a family of her own to lavish her love upon—and to feel like she belonged.

Jared said nothing, but continued to watch her handle the baby, his gaze flicking back and forth between Jenny and Jamie. His expression remote, he remained silent.

Jenny grew nervous, self-conscious. She put down the bottle to raise Jamie to her shoulder, wishing she could think of something to say to fill the silence. What would a well-traveled man like him wish to talk about?

"For someone who just teaches kids, you seem quite competent with a baby," he commented.

She shrugged. "I spent a lot of time at the Home rocking babies. I watched what the housemothers did and picked up pointers. But feeding and changing is about my limit. So no getting sick, little one," she said to Jamie.

"You recommend we buy a rocking chair and crib and clothes for the baby. Anything else?"

Jenny eyed him uncertainly. "Are you planning to buy this furniture or just rent? If she's here for only a couple of weeks, it seems silly to spend so much money. There're bound to be rental places where you can get a crib and rocker."

"Money's not an issue. We'll buy what you think she needs. Someone can always use it when we're done. So what else would we need?"

Jenny felt a tug of happiness at his including her in the decision.

"We'll see as we go along. I'll get some more formula when I do the grocery shopping. Do you feel up to going out this morning?" she asked when Jamie settled down to drinking her bottle again. "You seemed to manage the inside stairs today."

Jared grimaced. "As long as I can take my time. A good night's sleep goes a long way. But I don't need to go. You know what she needs, you pick out the things."

"It's your money. You need to make sure you get value for your dollars."

"I trust you," he said.

"I don't know how much you want to spend or the kind of furniture you'll want. You need to pick it out," Jenny insisted.

"I don't want to go."

"We all have to do things in life we don't want to," she said with some asperity.

Honestly, he acted as if she was demanding he do something illegal, not accompany her on a mere shopping trip where she'd be spending his money.

"Great, now you sound like my father," Jared said. "I don't need platitudes. Besides, I'm not up for another taxi ride."

"I have my car. We'll put the baby in the back and you can sit in the front. Push the seat all the way back and stretch out your leg," she offered. "Where did you get that infant carrier? It doubles as a car seat, doesn't it?"

"Jim bought everything a child could possibly need before she was born. He was so delighted with her. Sohany insisted on naming the baby after Jim. I suspect she always believed he'd return to the States at some point and leave them behind."

"Instead, they both died. It's so sad. What happened to the rest of the things he bought?"

"I had one of the men from the field office donate everything we couldn't bring home. Too expensive to ship it Stateside. It's cheaper to buy new stuff."

"If you get a good quality crib, you can save it for a child of your own."

"I have no intention of marrying or having kids," he said easily.

"You can't travel all your life. At some point, don't you want to establish roots? Have a family? Settle down?"

"Can't see that far ahead. Maybe when I'm sixty. But I'm willing to bet that's what you want—a home and a family. I'm surprised you're still single."

Jenny leaned forward, fussing with the baby, hoping her hair would hide the stain of color she felt rise in her cheeks. She didn't want to have to confess the situation that had prompted her acceptance of the summer job.

"Hit a nerve?" Jared persisted.

She glared at him. "I do want a family someday. Isn't that rather normal for someone who has no one? I don't think there's anything wrong with that."

"Nothing. I'm just surprised some man in Whitney hasn't already made an offer."

"There's more to marriage than just receiving an offer. I want to be loved."

Jared looked puzzled. "Isn't that usually what happens in marriage—at least at the onset?"

"Not if you're asked in order to be a surrogate parent," she snapped.

"Ah, the awkward incident?"

"You know, Mr. Montgomery, I was hired to watch the baby, not answer an inquisition." He was quick. How long before he found out all the embarrassing details?

He smiled slowly, his eyes dancing in amusement. "I didn't know women still blushed these days."

Jenny wanted to run from the room, hide in the bathroom until her cheeks were as pale as snow. But handicapped with a baby in her lap, she held her ground. Raising her head haughtily, she longed for scathing words that would put the man in his place. Whatever that place was.

He had the nerve to laugh!

"At least now I'll know when I've crossed the line. My father is usually the one called Mr. Montgomery. I suspect you'll use that to advantage if you get miffed," Jared said, that lopsided smile almost melting her anger.

"Miffed? You pry into my private affairs and then expect me to be only miffed?"

"Annoyed? Mad as a hornet?" he offered helpfully.

His teeth were white against his tan, Jenny noted. Her heart began to flutter when he directed that sexy grin her way. Anger forgotten, she clutched her resolve to get over the attraction she felt around him. He was far more dangerous to her equilibrium than Tad had ever been. After the bruising her heart had taken with her former fiancé, she couldn't allow herself to rebound into Jared Montgomery's path. There was no future there. He'd just made that abundantly clear.

Deciding to take charge of the situation, Jenny rose with the baby. "I'll change Jamie and we can leave. I parked on a side street, but can bring the car around to Decatur if you like."

"Okay, I'll give it a shot. But not just yet. I'm expecting a call. We'll leave around eleven. And you don't need to bring the car here. I'm sure I can manage a few blocks, if I can make it down the stairs."

Jared's gaze drifted down her legs and Jenny again felt that shock of heat spiral inside. How could a mere look evoke such a reaction? Fleeing for the safety of the upstairs bedroom, she wondered how she would make it through the next few weeks without revealing a hint of that strong attraction.

Jared listened to Jenny rush up the stairs. The floors on the third floor had only scatter rugs. He could clearly hear her footsteps as she stormed into the spare bedroom. Shaking his head, he closed his eyes briefly, picturing her surprised expression, the flush of color in her cheeks. Teasing her was fun. Who'd expect anyone these days to blush at the slightest comment? How would she react if he said something suggestive?

He turned his head to gaze out through the French doors. He really didn't want to follow that line of thought! His imagination had run rampant last night. Time to put things into perspective. She was here to watch the baby, that was all.

It was a beautiful day. Before long, it would grow hot and humid. Nothing like the heat of the desert, but sultry and heavy. He'd be home for at least four more weeks, or until his ankle healed and he obtained a clean bill of health from the company doctor. Maybe longer if he hadn't found a place for Jamie by then.

He listened to the muffled movement upstairs. Could he last four weeks sharing the apartment with Jenny Stratford? Last night's imaginings had spilled over to this morning. Eating breakfast with her hadn't been easy.

His fingers still itched to touch that silky hair. The urge to kiss her had risen again during breakfast. When powdered sugar clung to her lips, he'd wanted to reach out and lick it away, then kiss her until she couldn't breathe.

Only common sense had kept him in his seat. The more he grew to know her, the more he suspected she was not the kind of woman for a quick fling. She had hearts and flowers and picket fences written all over her.

Though she surprised him when she'd been thrown off with the comment about her looks. She'd seemed genuinely amazed. Who did she hang out with that no one had told her what a knockout she was?

But then, women were contrary and confusing creatures. Maybe he'd test the waters. A brief affair over the summer could suit them both. Each of them had plans for the fall, a natural ending to an affair without the usual sticky emotional entanglement that lingered.

And there was no danger of becoming trapped in marriage. He was too wary for that. Not after Andrea. Jared never intended to make a similar mistake.

He wondered what kind of mistake it might be to give in to the urges that filled him since he first laid eyes on Jenny. To wrap her pale blond hair in his fist and draw her close enough to kiss. To taste her unique, special flavor, to touch that flawless skin, to explore the pulsating excitement that shimmered between them. How experienced was she? She was old enough to have been around a bit, but her wide-eyed enthusiasm made her seem far too innocent.

The attraction couldn't be all one-sided. Hadn't she looked at him like he looked at her? Or was it only wishful thinking on his part?

He frowned. It had been a while since he'd been involved with anyone. Was he misreading the signs?

He struggled to rise. He'd placed a call to the home office here in New Orleans, wanting an update on the situation at the site. When were they going to get back to him? He needed to focus on business and forget the pretty nanny he'd hired.

Chapter Six

"We're ready." Jenny came down the last couple of steps shortly before eleven.

Jared looked up, annoyed he'd been thinking so hard he hadn't heard her descent. Glancing at her, he paused as he reached for the crutches. Pink tinged her cheeks, her blue eyes sparkled. She bounced the drowsy baby gently, looking full of anticipation and excitement. Would she look that way if he kissed her?

"We need to take the baby carrier and a baby bag with formula, bottles and clean diapers," Jenny said as she placed the baby in the carrier. "There, munchkin, how's that? We're going for a ride and shopping. It's an activity you'll love as you get older."

"Don't start her this young," Jared murmured, watching Jenny fuss over the baby. There was something so right about the ritual. Her touch was gentle and loving. The infant gazed up at her with wide dark eyes. Did she have a clue to what Jenny was saying?

Her mother had spoken limited English, had probably talked to Jamie in Arabic. Could the baby tell the difference? Did she wonder where her parents were or could babies notice differences like that at two months, he wondered.

Jenny flashed a bright smile. "Why not? Practice makes perfect. I'll just be a sec. Did you get your call?"

He nodded. She'd stayed upstairs all morning.

Jenny whirled around gathering all the items she wanted to take. The soft-sided diaper bag bulged when she slung it over her shoulder. Her handbag hung from the other shoulder. Gingerly balancing both, she leaned down to pick up the infant carrier.

"Can you manage the stairs carrying her?" Jared asked, wondering what he'd do if she couldn't. He was going to have a hard enough time getting himself down.

"Sure. I'll hold the carrier by the handle and hold to the railing with my other hand. They're steep, though. Can you manage?"

"I came up, didn't I?"

"Going down looks harder," she retorted. "Is this some kind of masculinity issue—refusing any offers of concern or assistance?"

"I'll manage," he said briefly.

"I'm sure you can manage anything you set your mind to" she said sweetly.

Jared wanted to issue an appropriate comeback to her sassiness, but she had already turned and headed out the door.

When the one opposite opened, Jared hesitated. He didn't need Mrs. Giraux watching him again.

She was dressed to go out, in a print dress complete with lace collar. She always wore a hat and carried a handbag. She nodded politely to him and then smiled at Jenny.

"Come see Jamie, Mrs. G.," Jenny said, setting down the diaper bag and holding up the baby carrier. "Isn't she sweet?"

"Indeed." The elderly woman peered at the baby and

smiled softly. "Very sweet. You'll have to bring her to visit."

"Sure thing. I'll check in this afternoon. Will you be home then?"

"Yes, I'm just going to the post office and then to the drugstore. I'll be home all afternoon."

"We're going out to buy baby furniture. I don't think we'll be long either," Jenny said.

Mrs. Giraux nodded once at Jared and headed down the steps. Jenny turned to pick up the diaper bag and caught Jared's questioning look. "What?"

"How do you know her?" he asked.

"We met yesterday. She's nice." Peering down the stairs, Jenny waited until the woman had walked out into the sunshine before continuing. "I think she's lonely. You know she's a widow and lives all alone. She doesn't have any children or close family."

"Always seems to disapprove of me," Jared muttered.

Jenny laughed. "You probably scare her—all that testosterone."

"What?"

She grinned cheekily and headed down the stairs. "Jamie and I'll wait for you in the sunshine. Don't be all day!"

Jared watched until Jenny and the baby disappeared through the lobby door, surprised by her sassy remark. Slowly he smiled.

Negotiating the stairs took longer than he anticipated. Jenny had been right. It was trickier going down on crutches than up. He was glad he'd already called his doctor about a walking cast. Crutches were all right while in the hospital, but he needed more mobility— especially with the stairs.

For a moment he thought about his parents' single-

levelhome in Whitney. He could have stayed there except he
didn't want anyone to get attached to Jamie. And he couldn't
explain about her background. His folks knew Margaret and
the children. They'd known Jim most of his life. While he loved
his mother, she was a talker—the risk of a slip was too great.
Better to take the heat of his parents' disapproval than risk
exposure at this point.

He reached the street door and pushed it open at long last.
Jenny was wandering back and forth in front of the building,
talking to the baby. Her hair gleamed in the sunlight, bright
with highlights. He noted every inch of her trim figure.
Topped off by that shiny hair. The image of running his hands
down the silky strands wouldn't shake loose. Especially after
her sassy comment at the top of the stairs.

"Ready?" she called when she spotted him. Hurrying over,
she shifted the carrier to her other hand. Her smile awakened
something inside. He wondered what it would be like to have
her greet him with that sunny smile every day. To reach up and
kiss him, letting her mouth move against his.

Dumb idea. He could never in a million years envision her
in the Middle East. And he wasn't staying in New Orleans—no
matter how enticing the thought of kissing Jenny was.

"This carrier is heavy. First thing we get is a stroller," she
said.

"Which way to your car?"

Talk of strollers and babies brought home the sense of
claustrophobia just thinking about settling down always
engendered. He needed to keep his distance. Neither Jamie nor
Jenny was in the running for a permanent place in his life. They
were ships passing in the night, so to speak.

"It's on Royal, we can cut through by the cathedral. It

won't take long."

Jackson Square bustled in the late morning warmth. Adventurous tourists braving the heat of the day were already chatting with the sidewalk artists and skirting the fortune tellers' tables. A mime performed his routine, and on the corner a small boy danced for coins. Across Decatur Street a trio of sidewalk musicians entertained the crowd at the Café du Monde. The familiar hustle and bustle impressed itself on Jared's mind. He was home. For a while.

The uneven flagstone paving proved treacherous and Jenny stepped carefully, keeping a wary eye on Jared. He noted her concern and wondered what she'd try to do if he slipped. He had to outweigh her by eighty pounds or more. And he didn't want to contemplate her falling beneath him. Gripping the handles harder, he made sure the crutches didn't skid.

"Stop hovering like a mother hen," he ground out

"I don't want you to fall."

"As if you could stop me if I did. I can take care of myself. You take care of the baby. Where's your car?"

"Not far now. Where do you keep yours?" she asked as they came out of the narrow alley beside the cathedral, past the old cemetery. It was cooler in the shaded passage than beneath the blazing sun in Jackson Square.

"Don't have one. I'm not home enough to warrant one. I usually take a cab if I need to go anywhere. But the Quarter has everything I usually want. It's a rare day I need to go anywhere that would require a car here. I have a company vehicle at the site."

"Your sister said you worked in the Middle East but not where precisely."

"For the last eleven months, the United Arab Emirates.

Before that Kuwait."

"So you haven't been home for eleven months?" she asked in disbelief. She rarely took a weekend trip. This was her summer for a big adventure—and Whitney was only one hundred and forty miles north.

"Actually it's been almost two years since I was home. When I finished my previous assignment, I took a swing through Germany instead of returning Stateside."

"You're gone a lot."

"It's what the job calls for."

"Could you get another job if you wanted to stay home?" she asked, pointing to a blue convertible. "That's mine."

He stopped and stared at the sporty car. "Doesn't fit my image of you," he said as she unlocked the passenger door.

"What would?"

"A minivan?" he suggested slyly.

She laughed. "That's for mothers with tons of kids to chauffeur around. I'm a swinging single. Not yet ready for the minivan brigade."

"How swinging?" he asked as he stopped by the door, crowding her, invading her space. Maybe he'd misjudged her. Maybe she was the type for a summer fling.

Jenny looked up and hesitated, her eyes widening slightly, a hint of pink creeping into her cheeks.

It was all Jared could do to refrain from leaning forward and kissing her on the spot.

"Swinging enough to buy a convertible," she said slowly.

Jenny couldn't move. He was too close. She could feel the heat emanating from his body. It seemed to encircle her, hold her captive. For a moment she wished she truly was a wild, carefree, swinging single.

Instead, her one claim to insanity and foolishness had been to buy this car two years ago—though she had never regretted it. She loved how she felt driving along with the top down.

She knew her limits, however. They were not wild enough to entice a man like Jared. But for a moment the thought of doing just that was mesmerizing.

What would it be like to reach up and kiss him? To feel that searing heat envelop her as his arms pulled her against him and plundered her mouth with his? To lean into that strong body, explore the differences between them, all the while discovering the realm of pleasure she was sure she'd find in his embrace.

"It's a great day, but I don't want to put down the top, the sun wouldn't be good for Jamie," she said, turning away before she did something stupid—like give in to the roiling emotions that churned through her. Or read more into his teasing comment that was truly there.

Jenny placed Jamie carefully in the back seat, fastening the baby carrier securely. When she stood up, Jared's gaze locked with hers. Heat darted through her. He'd been watching her the entire time. She didn't know whether to act outraged or flattered.

Secretly, she hummed inside.

"Can you manage?" she asked stiffly. It was hot enough in New Orleans without her own body growing warmer every time she encountered Jared's gaze. How could he still look so cool, so calm? What would it take to shake the man up just a little?

He nodded looking as if he read her mind. "Sure, piece of cake."

She went around the car and slid in behind the wheel. By

the time she had calmed down enough to start the engine, Jared had maneuvered himself and his crutches into the car and closed his door. Jamie seemed content in the back.

"Where to?" she asked, flicking the air- conditioning on to high.

"Down Canal Street, to the right. We'll hit one of the major department stores. They'll have the biggest selection."

The outing took on a surreal feeling for Jenny when they entered the large department store a few minutes later. She glanced at Jared from the corner of her eye. Anyone looking at the three of them would immediately assume they were a happy family out on a shopping expedition. Her dream had simmered for so long. Would it ever come true?

"Don't you get tired of traveling?" she asked as they stood waiting for an elevator.

Jared looked down at her, as if giving serious consideration to the question. "Not so far."

"It seems a bit much, constantly moving from one place to another. I mean a vacation or long trip is one thing, but to live out of a suitcase all the time sounds awful."

He shrugged. "I'm used to it. I have base housing. I don't live out of a suitcase."

"Don't you want a more stable home?"

The doors slid open. Stepping into the elevator car, Jenny shifted the baby carrier. She had no idea babies could be so heavy—especially when so tiny.

"I have a home—the apartment."

"Right. There are no pictures on the walls, few books, no magazines, nothing that gives it any personality or comfort. It's cold and impersonal. You might as well stay in a hotel."

"Cheaper than a hotel."

Jenny stared at the floor indicator, knowing she'd been rude with her scathing remark about his home. But it was so sterile. Compared to her own place, it positively cried out for some color, something to warm it up. Plants would help. Paintings, rugs on the floor. She sighed. He hadn't hired her to decorate his apartment. She'd be lucky to get the rocking chair.

"Would you mind if I got a few plants for the balcony?" she asked, tempted to do so even if he said no.

They stepped off onto the fourth floor and headed to the far right where the baby department was located.

"Plants?"

"You know, some flowers, for color and fragrance. Jamie would like that. Babies like to look at bold colors."

She suspected he would have more difficulty refusing something for Jamie than for her.

"They'll just die when I go," he said.

"I could take them home with me when I leave."

"Do what you want to the place, I don't care," Jared said carelessly.

That much was obvious, she thought. But she kept her thoughts to herself. Or so she hoped.

"Now, now, teacher, don't get that look. If you want to get some things for the apartment for the few weeks you and Jamie will be there, have at it. Just don't ask me for any input. The place suits me fine the way it is. I'm not much on decorating."

Jenny nodded, already starting a mental list of everything she'd like to see. She'd make sure she bought things with her own money, then she would be able to take them home as a reminder of her summer in New Orleans.

Her spirits rose. It would be a challenge—spend little, yet make the apartment more homelike.

Upon reaching the baby department, a stroller was the first item she selected. Grateful to be relieved of the weight of the baby carrier and Jamie, Jenny placed her in the new stroller while they moved on to cribs. Before they finished selecting one, Jamie began to fret.

"She's probably hungry," Jenny said, pushing and pulling the stroller gently to induce a rocking motion. "And we have lots to buy. Including the rocker, don't forget."

"A rocker doesn't come under the heading of needs," Jared said, raising and lowering one side of a crib.

The saleswoman smiled sympathetically at Jenny. "They're a wonderful piece of furniture, and you can use it for years. Especially soothing for babies."

"I won't need it for years," Jared replied, moving on to another crib.

"I'll buy it and take it with me when I return home," Jenny put in.

At the startled look on the saleswoman's face, she knew the lady had immediately altered her conclusion that they were a normal, happy family.

Jared scowled at her. "We're supposed to be buying a crib. Which one do you think is best?"

"I like the oak one. The slats are too close together for a baby to get caught between them."

"Actually all are designed with safety features in mind," the salesclerk interposed.

"Okay, we'll take it," Jared said.

Jamie's cries increased in volume.

"Shh, shh, honey. We'll eat in a minute." Jenny rocked the stroller harder.

"I'll take care of the purchases, you find somewhere to feed her," Jared ordered.

Jenny glared at him. "Don't forget the bumper pads, sheets, blankets, extra diapers and some new clothes for her. And I still want a rocker."

"For heaven's sake, I don't know what you're even talking about."

His look of baffled frustration would have been comical if she wasn't concentrating on coming up with a convincing reason to buy a rocking chair.

"Fine, then you find some place to sit and you feed her while I get the things we need!" she said, exasperation rising.

Jared looked almost panicked. "I don't know how to make her stop crying. What if the bottle isn't what she wants?"

"She's hungry, trust me. Feeding her isn't that hard. It's that or get the rest of the stuff yourself."

"I don't know what to get," he said glaring back.

"You're the designated daddy, figure it out"

Jared opened his mouth, but closed it firmly when he realized the saleswoman was watching them with fascinated eyes.

"And just where do I find a place to sit and feed her?" he asked quietly, his eyes promising retribution at a later time.

Jenny knew when to retreat. She looked around, hoping to find a chair Jared could sit on to feed Jamie. Obviously he couldn't manage her and the crutches at the same time. The baby's screams were starting to attract attention from the other shoppers.

"The furniture department is on the next floor. I'm sure the salespeople there would let you try out one of our rockers," the saleswoman offered helpfully.

Jenny smiled in triumph. "Perfect I'll get them settled and

be right back for the rest of the things we need." Whirling the stroller around, she headed for the elevator.

Jared followed her, his expression dark.

"Do you know that woman?" he asked when he caught up to Jenny by the elevator doors.

"Who, the saleswoman?"

"Yeah. How convenient of her to suggest I try out a rocker while feeding the baby. Are you two in collusion?"

Jamie's wails grew louder.

"Shh, babykins. Daddy will feed you in just a minute."

"I'm not her daddy," Jared snapped.

"Except on the birth certificate. And until you unload her on someone else," Jenny said, pushing the stroller into the empty elevator. The baby's cries sounded even louder in the confines of the small space. Jenny reached out and picked her up, cuddling her against her breast patting her back in an effort to sooth her.

"I'm not unloading her on anyone. I'm trying to find her a good home," Jared said in exasperation.

"Hush little one, hush, hush. Soon you can eat. We brought you a bottle. Shh." She ignored him, trying to calm the baby.

Moments later Jared was ensconced in one of the larger rockers, bottle in hand, holding the tiny girl against his chest.

Jenny stared at the two of them for a moment caught up unexpectedly by the image. Somehow Jared looked even more masculine in contrast to the tiny creature gazing up at him with her wide dark eyes. Jamie's little hand rested on Jared's large one. The contrast was startling. Feeling oddly touched at the sight, Jenny spun around before she made a fool of herself. She was given to tearing up at the most inopportune times, and she refused to do so before Jared!

She was a sucker for men who watched over children—babies especially. It strengthened the masculine image somehow. Throughout history men had cared for their families, through hunting or tilling, or later in occupations that earned money to buy necessities. But they were also protectors keeping everyone safe. And holding the tiny baby gave her a glimpse of that protection. Jared might deny feeling anything special for his friend's baby, but he looked strangely right holding her.

It took Jenny longer than she anticipated to find all the things she wanted to get. She explained the situation to the saleslady—that she had been hired to watch Jamie for the summer; that Jamie and Jared had just returned from the Middle East and had no baby things at home. The woman was delighted to join Jenny in finding just the right items.

Looking at the stack as the woman began totaling everything up, Jenny began to wonder if she'd gone overboard. If so, she had no doubt Jared would clearly let her know.

When she returned to the furniture department, Jared sat in the rocker, gently pushing the chair back and forth. Someone had found an ottoman for his injured ankle and it was propped up. Jamie lay on his chest, her tiny head nestled beneath his chin, her eyes tightly closed.

Jenny couldn't help smiling when she saw them. She wished she could take a picture with her phone. Probably not something Jared would like.

"Everything okay?" she asked wondering how anyone could not be captivated by a baby.

"She finished eating a long time ago. I tried to keep her awake, but she fell asleep."

"Babies sleep a lot. And she's probably still adjusting to the time zone changes. Did you burp her?"

"Yes. I do know that much about babies. Patti has two kids and I saw both when they were babies. For some reason, she thought I was dying to hold them and would foist them off on me at the weirdest times."

"You look great holding Jamie," she said as she picked the baby up and gently placed her back in the stroller.

Jared looked at her sharply—had she meant anything by that remark?

It hadn't been as bad as he'd thought, feeding and holding little Jamie. He'd fed her once before, on the trip home, but the flight attendants had taken better care of her on that journey.

He'd been surprised at her size, so tiny. But she was a scrapper, he thought proudly. He could still hear her cries ringing in his ears. No doubting her lung power.

Her gaze had fastened on to his as she ate, her little hand had gripped a finger and held on tightly, her strength surprising him. When finished eating, she had squirmed around on his chest, as if wanting to crawl or get up and walk.

What did the future hold for this child? She was so young and innocent. She had so much to learn. For a moment he fervently wished all the best for his friend's daughter. Jim would never see her first steps, never hear her call him Daddy. Of course he'd had that privilege with his other children. But Jared knew Jim had equally loved this baby.

"I had the clerk stack everything at the counter. She's ringing up the total now. They'll deliver the crib tomorrow and set it up. It cost extra, but you aren't up to it and it's too heavy for me," Jenny said straightening.

"I can set it up." Jared rose and stepped away from the

rocker.

Jenny looked at it longingly. Did she have any idea how expressive her face was?

"They can deliver the rocker when they deliver the crib," he said as he headed for the elevator.

Her smile about blew him away. "Thank you! You'll love it. And it will help so much when feeding Jamie. If you don't want it when we leave, I'll buy it from you."

He nodded, frowning.

Thanks were great.

He'd rather have had a kiss.

Chapter Seven

By late afternoon, Jenny was almost as tired and cranky as Jamie. The baby fussed, nothing would please her. Jenny knew she ought to be sleeping undisturbed in a cool, quiet room, but it had been a day for running around and they still had to unload the car when they reached the apartment. And, she had not yet gone grocery shopping.

After the baby supplies had been purchased, Jared had directed her to the hospital where his doctor agreed to provide a walking cast. Changing casts had taken longer than expected, and the new one still needed to harden overnight. The doctor had insisted on a complete exam, which extended the time even longer.

But it was worth it. Tomorrow Jared would graduate from crutches to a cane and the walking cast.

They'd eaten a late lunch in a small café near Tulane University, not far from the hospital. The New Orleans garden district was ablaze with colorful petunias, dahlias and fragrant roses. Huge, lofty old oaks and elms shaded lawns, giving the feeling of permanency and strength. Gray Spanish moss dripped from some of the older trees, a common sight in humid Louisiana.

Jenny would have loved to spend the afternoon pushing

Jamie in her stroller, wandering up and down the old sidewalks staring at the old homes to satisfy her love for color and beauty. Impossible today with Jared unable to join them. Maybe she'd bring the baby another day.

"Tomorrow I'll call my attorney and see what he has to say about finding a family for Jamie," Jared said as they headed back to the apartment, the late afternoon traffic already crowding the streets.

Jenny glanced at him. He'd not mentioned it all day. She had pushed the idea to the back of her mind and didn't like him bringing it up again.

"Are you going to vet this home you'll be giving her to? Check out the potential parents to make sure they'll take good care of her? What if they don't?"

"Of course they'll be checked out," Jared said patiently. "Arthur will see to it."

"Arthur being?"

"Arthur Perkins. He's been my attorney for years. We played football together back in high school."

"You have a real network of longtime friends, don't you?" she asked. "Jim, now Arthur."

"That's about it. I haven't kept in touch with many others. I'm gone too much," he said, slamming his foot to the floor of the car as if he could assist Jenny in stopping suddenly behind a car.

"Relax, I saw him in plenty of time," she said, bringing the car to a stop.

"I don't usually let anyone but a cab driver drive me," he murmured. "Now I remember why."

She laughed. Then she flicked a glance at him.

"I bet neither your friend nor Jamie's mother thought

you'd give away their baby," she said.

"And I bet neither Jim nor Sohany expected to be dead by now. What am I supposed to do with a two-month-old infant? I can't take her with me to oil fields. What kind of life would that be for her? I'm trying to do what I think's best for her. And being dragged from pillar to post all over the world isn't it."

"Maybe you should think about getting a job closer to home," she suggested.

Jared glared at her. "Maybe you should remember I hired you to watch the baby, not to advise me on how to live my life. Not that it's any of your business, but I tried that route once before. It didn't work. I like my life the way it is. I'm not going to get trapped in a relationship that keeps me tied to one spot—to become so dissatisfied with life that all I do is constantly complain. To discover no matter what I do, how hard I work, I can't satisfy anyone!"

Jenny blinked. "No one said you had to do that. But I think you'd want to do the best to honor your friend's wishes, especially when you promised him you'd take care of her."

"I didn't mean I'd raise her. She's my responsibility, I'll discharge that responsibility as I see fit." Jared looked at Jamie, his expression cool. "I'd think you'd consider a happy home the best thing for her. Didn't you always wish for one?"

"Touche. Yes, I did want a home while growing up— complete with loving parents, family traditions, grandparents. The whole works. You can provide that for her."

"I am by finding that perfect home for her."

End of discussion.

Jenny wondered what he'd been talking about when he said he'd tried that once. Obviously he'd been married. What happened?

She should have asked Patti more questions about her brother. But the baby had been of more interest when she'd learned of the job.

Even then, she hadn't expected to be so drawn to the baby in the back seat. She hated the thought of Jared giving her away as casually as he might give away an unwanted Christmas gift.

It was irrational, she knew, but she thought he should raise his friend's baby. There had to be some way he could do that.

Her lack of understanding for his position probably came from being an orphan herself—of having no one who'd known her parents be a part of her life. For all intents and purposes, she'd arrived on planet earth at age four when her life at the children's home had begun.

She didn't want the same legacy for Jamie.

"You were married?" she asked as they waited at a traffic signal. She couldn't resist that question. His comment raised her curiosity too high to ignore.

"Yes, years ago. It didn't work. I should have known better from my old man."

"Your father?"

Jared leaned back in the seat, resting his head against the neck support. "All my life I remember him complaining how being married ended his chance to see the world. How much more he could have done if he didn't have my mother and sister and me to provide for. How he'd been too young when he married, and now he was stuck."

"Your father told you that?"

"Me and anyone else who would listen. He was always ranting about it."

"Gee, I bet that makes you and your mom and sister feel

special. And he keeps saying it?"

Jared turned his head lazily. "Why not? It's the way he feels."

"Why not? If I were your mother, I'd bop him one. If he didn't like being tied down, why didn't he leave?"

"He's a man who stands behind his commitments."

"No matter whom he hurts in the process? Great. And that was your role model? I'm surprised you tried marriage at all."

"Yeah, me too, now. I thought we'd be different. Only, it turned out even worse than with my folks."

"How?"

Jared was quiet for so long, Jenny wondered if he would say anything further. She almost jumped in surprise when he again spoke.

"Andrea and I practically grew up together. We went to the same college. Then got married. But Andrea changed after that. Suddenly the things we talked about changed. She wanted everything a certain way, no compromise in her at all. Nagged me to death to get her own way."

He looked at Jenny. "We divorced after only two years. So now I can say I've been there, done that. No kids, so I was spared my father's fate."

Jenny shivered despite the day's heat. He sounded so cold so uncaring.

"I decided after my divorce that I was going to see the world. I was going to do what it took to go where I wanted, when I wanted and experience life," Jared said, no apology in his tone.

"So, nothing to tie you down," Jenny said, understanding a bit better his strong conviction to do things his way. It wasn't her way, though.

"Right."

"No one to share the good times with, no one to buy Christmas presents for, or go to Mardi Gras with. No one to take care of you if you're sick or tired. No one to come home to at night and shut the world away and find a world of your own."

He laughed. "I knew you were romantic."

"Those things are important to me. Laugh if you want, but I feel sorry for you."

Jared sat up at that. "Sorry for me? Honey, I've been places you've never dreamed of. Seen a dozen different cultures, eaten a hundred varieties of foods—"

"Spare me the travelogue. I'd like to visit some places in the world, but first I want a home and roots. And someone to share my life with. Don't you ever get lonely?"

"We want different things. You'll settle for some man to cook for, clean up after and be grateful because you have roots."

"At least I'll know I'm valued for myself. Who values you?"

"My employer for one," Jared shot back.

"Nope. Your company values your services, same as the school board values my teaching skills. I'm talking about being valued for yourself alone. If you don't show up for work one day, your employer will miss you—for the services you perform. But who will care about you if something happens?"

Jared stared out the front windshield. Jenny's words hit hard. He took a quick look at his life. She had some point to that comment and it made a kind of sense. He had no one besides his immediate family who really cared about him. He visited as little as possible. He couldn't really say he and his parents were close. Or that his sister Patti was even aware of what he did.

Jim had known and cared.

But Jim was dead.

He had no other close friends. He'd cut himself off from childhood buddies with his constant traveling. And being assigned a few months in different locations didn't make it easy to develop deep friendships at work, either. Before he settled in anywhere, he was moving to the next location.

"I still need to buy groceries. Where do you normally shop?" Jenny asked as they approached the French Quarter.

"At the market on Decatur Street. It's close enough to walk. Might as well find whatever parking place you can and walk from the apartment."

He stopped thinking about the way he lived his life. It suited him. As soon as he was fit, he'd return to the U.A.E. and plunge back into the work that awaited.

And in no time he'd forget the pretty blond woman who wanted a family and home and all the things he'd renounced.

Chapter Eight

Shopping at the market a half hour later, Jenny was relieved to be on her own for a little while. She hadn't wanted to keep the baby up any longer. Jamie was already sound asleep in the makeshift crib when Jenny left. Jared had agreed to watch her—not that Jenny expected the child to do anything but sleep.

Still, it was a concession on his part. She knew Jared was in pain. She'd seen him down two more of those pain pills at the hospital. He was trying to do too much, too soon. He'd only been released from the hospital a few days before. And the time they'd spent shopping, then changing the cast had to increase his discomfort.

Maybe she shouldn't have insisted he accompany her on the shopping expedition.

Not that he'd complained. She had never heard him complain about anything–not about the discomfort he had to be in, nor the circumstances that left him with full responsibilities of an infant.

Glad to escape Jared's disturbing proximity, she dawdled as she picked over the fresh vegetables, trying to plan a few meals in her mind. She needed to get organized and would be in a much better position once she sorted things out. But now she needed to get enough food to tide them over a couple of days. By then she'd have a better idea of what he liked.

And not just in the food department. She found herself floundering for things to say. If she didn't totally alienate him with her inappropriate comments, she went to the other extreme—tongue-tied and gauche. Maybe if she had a clue to his likes and dislikes, she'd be able to carry on a reasonable conversation.

Or maybe she should fill every day with activities that would be far too difficult for a man wearing a cast to participate in. Keep her distance and give herself time to get over that heart stopping, shivering awareness that plagued her around Jared.

But that would likely mean activities too much for a baby, too.

The thought of spending the lazy summer days lounging around the balcony, of taking Jamie for walks along the Mississippi river bank, or sitting in the sun in the Square held far too strong an appeal, especially when Jared featured in every scenario.

Summer was short—make the most of it, she advised herself.

Staring off into the distance for a long moment, she wondered just how she could make the most of it.

She wished she dared to explore that strong attraction. But she hadn't a clue how to let him know she might like a kiss or two. How did a woman convey that without looking like a brazen hussy?

And save face if he didn't share that interest?

She wouldn't be able to stay if she made a fool of herself.

Sighing, she knew she had to come up with something and

soon, or he'd drive her crazy.

One kiss. That would be enough. Surely she was up to figuring out a way to finagle one kiss.

When she reached the apartment, Jenny carried the two bags of groceries up the steep stairs. There had to be a better way to shop besides visiting the market every other day. But without the benefit of her car, she couldn't carry home more than two bags at a time. With parking at such a premium in the Quarter, she wondered if she could get food delivered.

Jared probably never thought about it, she grumbled as she climbed the steps. From the looks of his barren cupboards, he ate out a lot. Of course, since he hadn't been in the country for almost two years, she wouldn't have trusted any food on the shelves anyway.

She put the bags down on the landing and fumbled with the unfamiliar lock. Opening the door quietly, she peered in. Jared was on the sofa, papers and folders spread around him and scattered on the rug. He'd obviously been reviewing something, but now his head rested on the back—he was sound asleep.

Gathering the grocery bags, wincing at the sound of paper being crushed, she closed the door and went quietly to the kitchen. In no time she'd put everything away.

Hearing a murmuring, she crossed to the wide dresser drawer they were using as a crib and scooped Jamie up. The baby regarded her with wide eyes, but made no sound now that she was held.

"Have you been a good girl while I was gone?" Jenny asked softly, cuddling the child close as she carried her upstairs. "We'll get all dressed up and go see if Mrs. Giraux is home. Want to go visiting?"

Quickly changing her, then preparing a bottle of formula, Jenny carried the baby to the door. One last glance at Jared showed he was still sleeping. Should she leave a note? No, they wouldn't be gone that long. He'd probably sleep through to dinner.

Studying him, she wondered if she could do anything to make him more comfortable. His chest rose and fell with his breathing. His face looking relaxed, his hair in that familiar disarray. His eyelashes made dark crescents against the tops of his cheeks. Some of the harsh edges seemed smoothed. A different facet of the man.

She looked her fill until Jamie grew restless with their stillness.

Shaking her head at her foolishness, Jenny kissed Jamie's cheek, breathing in her sweet baby scent, and stepped out onto the landing, closing the door soundlessly behind them.

Two seconds later, she knocked gently on their neighbor's door.

"You brought the baby! How nice. Do come in." Mrs. Giraux looked ready for company, her summer dress a formal contrast to the casual shorts Jenny wore.

"I hope we aren't coming at an inappropriate time," Jenny said, stepping into the apartment.

"Oh no, dear, not at all inappropriate. I'm delighted you came. As the afternoon waned, I was beginning to wonder if you would. Do sit down. Isn't she precious!"

Jenny smiled at the older woman and sat on the sofa. When Mrs. Giraux sat primly beside her, she held out the baby.

"Want to hold her?"

"Oh, I couldn't. I don't know a thing about babies. Mr. Giraux and I were never blessed." From the wistful tone in her voice, Jenny knew it had been a big disappointment.

"She won't break. Good grief, if Jared could manage, you certainly can. The man hasn't the first clue about babies."

Despite that, the image of him holding Jamie in the rocking chair that morning came to mind. He might not have a clue, but he was willing to try.

Gently she laid Jamie in Mrs. Giraux's arms. "Her name is Jamie. She's two months old and brand new to America. She was born in the United Arab Emirates."

"She's a wee little thing, isn't she?"

"Right now, but with some judicious feeding, she should gain some weight soon, don't you think?" Jenny asked.

"I would expect so. What a good baby!"

Jenny laughed. "You won't think so when she gets hungry. I brought a bottle in case. She was screaming earlier—this morning. I'm surprised you didn't hear her."

"The walls of this old place are well built. I heard nothing," Mrs. Giraux said.

Jenny glanced around. She'd stopped by to introduce herself yesterday afternoon but hadn't really taken a good look. While a bit too formal for her tastes, she could tell Mrs. Giraux took a great deal of pride in keeping her home immaculate.

Spotting framed photographs of children on one of the tables, she rose and went to study them, picking up one.

"Cute little boys."

"Samuel's nephews. Those photos are from when they were little. Goodness me, they're in their fifties now. I haven't seen them in such a long time," she said wistfully.

"Why not? Where do they live?"

"Up north. When Samuel was alive, we used to drive up there every three years to visit his brother and his family. But he's been gone for more than ten years now. And the journey is too much for me alone."

Jenny put the frame back on the table, feeling sad. Here was someone else who would have loved to have had a huge family and hadn't. She shivered. She didn't want to end up at the end of her life with no one around to share memories and holidays.

"Did you and Samuel live here?" Jenny asked, moving to study some of the other pictures.

"Oh no, dear. We had a lovely home not too far from the university. But after he passed on, I couldn't keep it up. The yard and all, you know. He always took care of hiring workers. I had such a lovely garden. And a woman came in to help me every day." She fell silent a moment, lost in memories.

Jenny waited patiently, feeling a kinship with Mrs. Giraux's loss. How sad to have had to leave the house she'd shared for so long with her husband.

Mrs. Giraux looked at her and smiled brightly. "But I like this apartment. I can sit on the balcony and watch the tourists. I can walk anywhere I want in the Vieux Carre, so I don't have the expense of a car. It's really quite a nice location."

Jenny looked to her balcony. It was filled with colorful flowering plants and a small wrought-iron chair padded with bright cushions placed near the railing. It was lovely. At least she'd brought some of the beauty from her garden. Jenny hoped it was enough.

Jamie began to fret.

"Oh, dear, she's upset," Mrs. Giraux said, looking flustered and distressed.

Turning quickly, Jenny saw Jamie was working herself up to start crying. She grabbed the bottle.

"I think she's getting hungry. You can feed her if you like."

"I should like that." Mrs. Giraux smiled and settled back, offering Jamie the bottle, never taking her gaze from her once the baby latched onto the nipple.

"Now while this little miss eats, why don't you tell me more about yourself. I was so pleased you stopped by yesterday, but you told me so little," Mrs. Giraux said.

Jenny settled on the chair opposite and began to tell her new neighbor about growing up in Whitney, about teaching the first grade and her fabulous summer job. Before Jamie finished eating, there was a knock on the door.

"Shall I get it?" Jenny asked, jumping up.

"Please, do. I can't imagine who would be coming to see me. I rarely get visitors. That's why your coming over is so special."

"I wondered where you had gone," Jared said when Jenny opened the door.

"I thought you'd sleep the rest of the afternoon. You looked like you were out for the count. How did you know to look for us here?"

"Who is it?" Mrs. Giraux called, trying to look over her shoulder to the door.

"It's Jared. Come on in." Jenny held the door wide.

He shook his head, catching a glimpse of the room.

"I don't need to come in, just wanted to make sure this is where you two were. I saw your purse on the kitchen table, so suspected you hadn't gone far. I remembered you said earlier you were coming over here."

"Come in, we're just talking. Mrs. Giraux is feeding Jamie."

"No—"

Jenny stepped closer and whispered urgently, "Do come in,

she rarely gets visitors and I think she would love to have us stay a bit."

Jared paused, frowning slightly, then he carefully maneuvered his crutches through the door. "Did anyone ever tell you you're bossy?" he asked in passing.

Jenny smiled brightly. "No. Sit down on the straight-back chair. It'll be easier for you to get up again," she said.

"So nice of you to drop by, Mr. Montgomery. Would you like a glass of sherry or something?" Mrs. Giraux asked. "As soon as the baby is finished eating, I can get us some refreshments."

"No, thank you. I'm taking pain medication and can't mix that with alcohol."

"Of course. What was I thinking of?" Flustered, she looked at Jenny.

"Isn't her home darling?" Jenny asked as she sank beside Mrs. Giraux and glanced around the apartment with a wide smile on her face. "I bet everything here brings a memory."

"Yes, my dear, that's true. Samuel and I furnished our house together. It was such a wrench to leave it. Most of the pieces remind me of happier days."

Jamie spit out her nipple and moved around.

"Do you think she's full?" the elderly woman asked in bewilderment. "There is still half a bottle of milk remaining."

"Probably has some gas in her stomach. Just raise her up on your shoulder. Wait, here, use this cloth to keep anything from getting on your lovely dress." Jenny arranged the baby and showed Mrs. Giraux how to rub her back.

"Being upright will help the air escape."

When the baby gave a burp, Mrs. Giraux beamed proudly.

Jenny laughed. "It's weird. We spend the entire first few

months of a person's life encouraging them to burp, then the rest of childhood discouraging it. I can tell you, first graders think there is nothing funnier than burping in class. Mostly the boys," she said glancing at Jared. "But the girls do their fair share."

Jared nodded, remembering when he'd been a kid. He had gotten a kick out of doing outrageous things to annoy his mother.

Glancing around the room, he shifted uncomfortably on the chair, feeling out of place. The place was so cluttered with delicate furniture, bric-a-brac and photographs in ornate frames that he wondered how Mrs. Giraux moved around without knocking into something.

He looked at the elderly woman patting Jamie's back and the young one beside her. Three generations sat on the sofa. None related, yet there seemed to be something between them. A woman's thing, he thought.

He hadn't wanted to stop and visit. He'd wanted to make sure Jenny was here. Which struck him as odd now that he watched her encourage his neighbor in her attempts to care for the infant. Jenny Stratford was perfectly capable of taking care of herself. She didn't need someone to look out for her.

"I was sorry to hear of your injuries," Mrs. Giraux said, looking at him.

"I'll be fine in no time," Jared said. She reminded him a little of his mother's mother. Grandmama Louise had been tiny, almost frail, yet had an iron will and a determination that had been stronger than steel.

"If I can do anything to help, do let me know," she said.

Jared opened his mouth to say he needed nothing, but Jenny caught his eye and shook her head slightly. Closing his mouth, he glared at her. Now what? Was he supposed to accept help from this frail elderly neighbor just to make her feel needed? He wouldn't inconvenience her.

Scowling, he looked away from the warmth in Jenny's eyes and stared out the opened French doors. He wasn't here to cater to women—at any age. The sooner he got his life back under control the better he'd like it.

Starting with taking charge now. He'd return to his own place and see about getting something to eat. Before he drew his crutches closer, however, Mrs. Giraux asked him about his work and before Jared knew how it happened, he'd spent more than a half hour discussing the fascinating aspects he found dealing with oil exploration and discovery.

Every time he glanced at Jenny, she was gazing at him as if enthralled. Someone should let her know that as a technique for capturing a man's attention, it couldn't be beat.

Again the thought of a summer affair rose. His fingers still itched to touch that champagne-blond hair. To feel the silky texture. To learn all the secrets she held.

Mrs. Giraux handed Jamie back to Jenny and rose. "I can fix some tea, or coffee, if you are not drinking sherry," she said starting for the kitchen.

"It's time we were heading back," he said, pulling the crutches closer. He'd be glad tomorrow when he could move on to the walking cast and a cane. At least he'd be more mobile.

"It's no trouble," she said.

"We've stayed long enough." Feeling closed in, he needed to get out. He rose and looked at Jenny."Time to start dinner, isn't it?"

She picked up the cue right away, he noticed.

"It is if we want to eat at a normal hour. Thanks for having us over, Mrs. G. It's been fun."

"Thank you for coming. Wait now, just a minute. I want you to take some macaroon cookies home. You two can eat them later." She bustled into the kitchen, returning in only a moment with a plate piled high with fresh macaroons.

"I enjoyed holding and feeding Jamie. Maybe you can come again soon," she said, patting Jamie's arm gently.

"Sure thing." Jenny quickly picked up the few things she'd brought with Jamie and took the plate of cookies. It was awkward, but easier for her than Jared. She smiled at Mrs. Giraux and was in Jared's apartment before he could work his way around the antiques and furnishings to get to the door. He nodded again to his neighbor and soon closed his own door behind him.

Chapter Nine

"She's lonely," Jenny said as she placed Jamie in the baby carrier.

Jared watched as she leaned over. He took a breath and forced himself to move out of the line of sight. He had other things to concern himself with besides being infatuated with the baby's nanny.

"She reminds me of visiting my grandmother when I was a kid. Grandmama Louise was tiny, too. And had more furniture than space in her house. I was always afraid I'd smash something."

"Maybe your grandmother also moved from a larger place to a smaller one. That's Mrs. G.'s problem. She moved from a house to that apartment. She probably found it impossible to give up any of the things she and her Samuel acquired during their marriage."

"Another reason for avoiding marriage," he said, walking across the room to the kitchen.

"You're so cynical. Why?" Jenny followed, placing the infant seat on the table, well away from the edge. She set the macaroons on the counter.

"Would you really want to live in a place with all that clutter?" he asked, opening the refrigerator and pulling out a can of soda. He held it up and raised his eyebrows in silent question. Jenny nodded and reached for it.

"Thanks. Not unless everything had meaning to me. Your place is a bit um, the other way, wouldn't you say?"

"At least I can walk through it without bumping into anything," he said, getting himself a soda.

"Well, what do you think, Jamie? Does Mrs. G. have too much stuff?"

Jared watched as Jenny talked with the little girl, acting as if Jamie could understand and respond. The baby seemed fascinated with Jenny, her big brown eyes following her every move. Her little legs kicked and her arms waved as if she was trying to communicate by kinetic energy.

Jenny looked up. "Does she look like her mother or her father?"

"I don't know. She looks like a baby to me."

"How can you be alert to all the variations in rock and ground signs to search for oil and not notice something as basic as that? Men, aren't they funny sometimes, sweetie?" she asked Jamie, giving her a kiss on her cheek.

Jared wished Jenny would give him a kiss—and not on the cheek.

He took a long drink of the cold soda, wishing it would cool off his thoughts.

Crushing his soda can, he tossed it into the sink, the last of the sweet beverage dribbling down the drain.

"Dinner anytime soon?" he asked.

"I'll fix something. Want to watch Jamie?"

"Isn't she going to sleep?"

"She can't sleep all the time. She seems alert and wide-awake now. She won't bite. You could even hold her. Babies need lots of touching and cuddling."

"Can't we just leave her in the baby carrier?"

"Mr. Montgomery." Jenny's eyes narrowed as she studied him. "You're not afraid of this baby, are you?"

His steely gaze met hers. "Of course not."

"Well, I don't want to just plunk her into a baby carrier and leave her. You can sit here and talk to me while I fix dinner. And you might as well hold her," Jenny said firmly.

"I have work to do."

"You're on medical leave," she countered, wondering why he put up such a fuss. "It's not like you have to finish a report and fax it back today, is it?"

"All right, give me the kid." He pulled out a kitchen chair and sat quickly, holding out his hands.

Gently Jenny placed Jamie in his arms. The little girl's eyes moved to study Jared. Her hands moved, batting air, connecting with his cheek from time to time.

"She likes you," Jenny said, beginning to prepare dinner.

It had been a long day and she was tired. A quick meal and then bed for her and Jamie. Surely Jared must be tired as well, despite his afternoon nap.

But when she glanced over at him, he didn't look tired. He was rocking back and forth in the chair, studying the baby in his arms. Jenny's heart almost melted. He was so big and stern looking, yet held Jamie with a gentleness that touched her.

"I bought some deli potato salad and planned to have grilled hamburgers, is that all right?" she asked as she took the meat from the refrigerator.

"Sure. Make two for me and make them big. We didn't get many burgers in the U.A.E."

"Tell me some more about living over there. I was

fascinated by what you told us at Mrs. G.'s."

"So it appeared. Don't go getting all starry-eyed about life in foreign countries. I like it, but it's not for everyone. Especially the desert."

"I guess not when you lose water for a week or have those sandstorms. Don't you miss the amenities we have here in the States?"

"Sometimes, but the cities there are every bit as modern as any here. It's just out at the site where we have to make do. Same as we would if we were on a rig in the Gulf, or up in some of the remote places in Alaska."

"I guess. How do you like your hamburgers?"

"Rare."

"Do all men like rare meat? Does that hark back to cavemen days when you dragged the mastodon to the fire, heated it a bit and gnawed it to the bone?"

"Charming picture," Jared smiled. "I can't speak for all men, but I like rare meat."

"So did Tad," she mumbled, slipping the patties beneath the broiler.

"Who's Tad?"

"No one important," she said breezily, her back to Jared. Why had she let that slip? After the embarrassment of discovering Tad had merely wanted a mother for his boys and really hadn't loved her, she should completely wipe his memory from her mind.

But it was hard. She'd been so happy, planning their future, imagining babies being born into their family, the activities they'd all do together. He'd known how much she wanted a family. To him, she guessed, it hadn't seemed like that big a deal, another child or two—as long as she was there to watch them all.

Jenny felt Jared's gaze, knew he was curious, but refused to say anything more. If he didn't already know about her stupid mistake, she certainly wasn't going to tell all.

"She looks a bit like Sohany around the eyes. Her eyes were dark," Jared said unexpectedly.

"What?" Jenny whirled around and stared at him. What was he talking about?

"Jamie—her eyes look like her mother. But her chin looks like it's going to be as stubborn as Jim's."

"You have to make sure she knows that when she's growing up."

His gaze met hers. "Maybe you should write these things down as I think of them. We can give the notes to the new parents. There's no telling how often I'll be back. What if they move or something?"

"You can keep in touch. Stop by to see her whenever you return home—if you're determined to go through with this."

"Of course."

Jared didn't like the fact she continued to challenge his decision. Patti had hired her to watch the baby temporarily, not lecture him on responsibility. Hadn't he taken Jamie away from a country where no one wanted her—where she would have had to go to an orphanage somewhere?

He'd make sure she had a good home.

Then his debt to his friend would be paid.

Jenny turned back to her preparations, her back ramrod straight. She made her thoughts abundantly clear. But it didn't matter, he wasn't changing his lifestyle plan just to please a woman he'd met less than twenty- four hours ago.

He jiggled the baby a little, trying to ignore the fact that it seemed a lot longer than twenty-four hours since he met Jenny. Maybe because he hadn't stopped thinking about her for more than a minute or two during the entire time.

When dinner was ready, Jenny took the baby and placed her in the carrier on the table so she could be with them while they ate.

The silence stretched out for endless minutes. At first Jared didn't mind. He was hungry and the hamburgers were delicious. What did she do to them to make them so tasty?

Or was it because it was his first dinner on American soil in so long that made them seem so special?

By the time he was halfway through his second hamburger, the silence was beginning to get on his nerves. In fact, he was surprised she could keep quiet so long. He pegged her as open, friendly and talkative.

"Good meal," he said, hoping to start the conversation ball rolling.

She nodded formally but refused to even look his way.

Jared felt a stirring of temper. Was she sulking because he wasn't going to provide a home for Jamie?

"If you plan to sulk all evening, maybe you should do it in your room," he said, his eyes on her.

Her gaze swung to his instantly. He could see fire flash in her eyes, hear the passion in her voice when she spoke.

"I'm not sulking! I'm trying to remember that you're my employer and not step over the line!"

"What line?"

He almost laughed—satisfied to have gotten a rise out of her. She was pretty when fired up. While she looked like a cool ice princess, she had enough fire and sass to warm any man.

Great, there he went again, thinking of her in terms that

were strictly off-limits.

She took a deep breath then hesitated a moment. Jared knew she was marshaling her thoughts.

Now what? He couldn't wait, the anticipation built with each passing second.

"If you aren't careful, you'll end up like Mrs. Giraux, alone in the world. Only in your case, you won't even have lovely memories to comfort you. What are you going to do when you're old and can't work anymore? Who will watch out for you, spend time with you, take care of you? How will you like spending holidays alone? Rarely having visitors. Living in the past?" she asked.

"Don't you think that's a few years away yet?"

She continued as if he hadn't spoken, "You don't want to get married, I guess I can kind of understand that. Unless you found some free spirit who liked to travel as much as you do, it sounds like it wouldn't work to begin with. But to turn your back on a child who could so easily become a part of your family, that doesn't make sense. Who will take care of you when you're old?"

"I do have parents and a sister, nephews," he mentioned, blood pumping through him as she warmed to her theme.

Color flew in her cheeks, her eyes sparkled and became even a deeper blue. The urge to reach over and kiss her grew proportionally with her impassioned lecture.

"Mrs. Giraux has nephews and hasn't seen them in years. Maybe you'll be luckier—"

"But you don't think so. Or is it you hope not?" he asked, wondering if he could rile her further.

Jenny looked at him in disbelief, caught the twinkle in his eyes. She opened her mouth to say something further, then snapped it shut, narrowing her own eyes in assessment

"Are you listening to me, or making fun?"

"I'm listening. And watching." And getting intrigued.

"What does that mean?"

"You're pretty when you're angry."

Dumbfounded, she stared at him for a long moment.

Slowly she stood and gathered her plate and glass. "I think this conversation is over," she said. Heading for the sink, she started in surprise when his hand shot out and closed over her arm.

"Don't run away."

"I'm not running away," she said disdainfully. "I'm finished. Time to do the dishes."

"Is our discussion ended?" he asked, his thumb rubbing lightly against her skin. It was as silky as he'd thought. He suspected every inch of her skin would be that soft. A hypothesis was well and good—scientists liked verification.

"You'll do whatever you want," she said. "You don't need my opinion."

Did her voice sound more breathless than normal? She cleared her throat. Maybe he made her nervous. He suspected this attraction couldn't be only on his part. Just what would she do if he said something outrageous?

"I don't know about doing whatever I want. I've wanted to kiss you all day and haven't yet," Jared said.

Chapter Ten

Her heart stopped. Jenny knew it had. Then it skipped a beat and began to race. Swirling heat enveloped her. A tingling awareness expanded to every cell, every nerve ending. She'd heard him correctly, hadn't she?

She licked her lips nervously, clutching the plate and glass. She stared into his warm blue eyes, saw the desire that sparked there. She didn't have to worry about making a fool of herself. He wanted to kiss her as much as she longed for a kiss from him.

"So the question now is do I continue to do whatever I want and kiss you or wait and see if you might be interested?" he asked. Releasing her arm, he pushed himself up until he stood beside her, balanced awkwardly on his good leg.

Tongue-tied, Jenny sought words to let him know she'd been fantasizing about kissing him since she first saw him. The fact he'd been thinking the same thing floored her.

Carefully placing the dish and glass on the table, she glanced at the baby to make sure she was all right then turned back to Jared, her heart pounding so hard she heard thunder in the blood that rushed through her veins.

Smiling brightly, she tried to cover up her nervousness, her shyness. She felt warm and mushy inside. And she'd never been so fully aware of herself as a woman before.

Clearing her throat again she boldly met his gaze.

"I guess one kiss couldn't hurt anything. I mean we don't know each other very well, yet we both know what the other wants. No false hopes on either side. This isn't leading to anything, right? One day I want someone to love, to marry; and you never do, so this isn't the start of—"

"Jenny, be quiet." His hands cradled her head, his fingers tangling in the silky heat of her hair. A woman could spend a long time just savoring the feelings that exploded with such a gentle touch.

Slowly he leaned forward, watching her. She knew her eyes widened slightly, then began to drift closed. Her hands gripped his wrists feeling the sinewy strength. She longed to feel his lips touch hers. Longed to see if the desire she'd glimpsed in him was matched within herself.

His breath brushed across her cheeks. Slowly she tried to relax.

How long had it been since she'd had a first kiss?

Would he stop at one?

One was all she'd wanted, now she knew it would never be enough. She should have factored lots more into the equation.

She could feel his body heat encompass her, surround her, ignite her own. She felt sheltered and cherished and on the edge of a huge precipice. She wanted to fling herself over into the unknown, discover what his mouth tasted like, how the strength of his body would feel when he enfolded her into his arms. Savor every minute sensation that cascaded through her like—

The strident ring of the telephone shattered the moment.

Her eyes flew open and she blinked as she stumbled back.

"Let it ring," he said, tightening his hold.

She stared at him, almost holding her breath. The phone continued to shrill in the silence that now engulfed them.

"It might be important." She pulled away and hurried to the living room to pick up the receiver.

"It's for you," she said, setting it down on the table by the sofa a second later.

Jenny's breathing hadn't returned to normal when she passed Jared and returned to the kitchen. Clearing the table, she did the dishes quickly, trying to ignore Jared's voice.

Shimmering waves of anticipation still filled her.

In a couple of seconds, she realized she could hear every word.

Including the exasperation that colored his tone.

The call was obviously from his mother.

Jenny giggled softly when she heard him argue with her, defending his stand to return to New Orleans instead of to Whitney, then back down and agree to have his parents come visit. He adamantly refused to travel to Whitney, citing his injuries as the reason. He then had to calm his mother's obvious worry about how badly he was injured.

Jenny wondered why he didn't want to go home.

He'd traveled from the Middle East on his own, managing Jamie and all their luggage. He could easily make the three-hour car trip to his parents' home.

Again she wondered why he hadn't stayed with them to begin with. He would have saved the expense of her salary for one thing. Probably would have been able to borrow baby furniture from Patti. The more she thought about it, the odder it seemed to insist on coming to New Orleans merely for fear Jim's wife would hear about Jamie. As far as she knew, the entire world believed the baby to be his.

Apparently his sister Patti and her family were at his parents. Jenny heard him thank her for finding a nanny for Jamie. Then he spoke with his father. She heard the reserved note in his voice when speaking with the older man. They obviously were not close.

By the time the call wound down, she'd straightened the kitchen. Time to prepare Jamie for bed. The baby was getting fussy and rubbing her face around her eyes.

"An early bedtime for both of us, pumpkin. Tomorrow your new crib will be here. Won't you like that?"

Jared remained on the sofa after he hung up, his long legs stretched out before him. He frowned, his gaze on his cast.

Looking up when Jenny walked in holding the baby, his expression didn't change. She could read nothing from it, either.

"I need to get her ready for bed," she said watching him warily. Her body still hummed with the sensations his touch brought. She swallowed hard, wishing the phone hadn't rung, wishing she'd had that one kiss she so yearned for.

But the moment had vanished. She had a fussy baby now to take care of.

"Are you coming back down?" he asked.

Slowly Jenny shook her head. "I think I'll turn in early, too. Jamie might wake in the night, so I need to sleep when I can. See you in the morning."

"I still want that kiss."

"I'm not sure that's such a good idea."

She regretted the interruption, but it had given her a little time to think things through as she'd washed the dishes. They had to live in close proximity for the next few weeks, no sense tempting fate.

And it wasn't as if there would be any future for the two of them together. Jared had made it very clear he was not interested in a long-term relationship—or marriage.

And Jenny very much wanted both one day.

"Doesn't that make it all the more fun?" he asked.

"It's tempting, that's for sure." He'd never know just how tempting! "Good night."

While she changed Jamie and settled her in her makeshift bed, Jenny could think of nothing else except their almost kiss. She could still feel his hands. The way he'd rubbed her hair like it was silk or something. Her mouth almost ached with longing. Why couldn't the phone have rung just sixty seconds later?

Slipping beneath the cool sheets on her bed a few minutes later and flicking off the light, she wished she were brave enough to march down the stairs and over to that sofa and tell him the heck with being a good idea—she was up for anything he wanted to do.

She could almost feel his lips against hers. Would his kisses be hot and fiery? She suspected Jared's kisses would be nothing like the platonic ones she'd received from Tad.

Moaning softly with the desire that seemed to fill her and spill into every cell, she curled up on her side and tried to think of something else. Anything else. She didn't want to keep dreaming about kissing Jared. She'd drive herself crazy.

Anyway, maybe she wouldn't like it.

Ha! Who was she trying to kid? There wasn't a woman on the planet who wouldn't enjoy being kissed by Jared Montgomery.

She was far more worried she would like it more than any kiss she'd ever had and would then crave more than one. And that definitely should not happen.

Tomorrow the baby furnishings would arrive. After she set up an area in her room for Jamie, she'd take the baby on a long walk. The stroller offered a certain amount of freedom and she'd take advantage of it. If she carefully planned her days, filled them with activities with the baby, she knew she could avoid the temptation of Jared Montgomery.

At least she hoped so.

Otherwise, she was in big, big trouble.

Chapter Eleven

Jenny was up, showered and dressed before seven the next morning. Jamie started to fuss while she was brushing her hair. Changing the little girl, Jenny crept down the stairs, afraid of waking Jared if he was using the sofa as a bed.

The living room was empty. The papers he'd been reading yesterday had been stacked in piles on the low table in front of the sofa. Relieved to postpone their next confrontation, Jenny carried Jamie into the kitchen while she prepared her bottle.

A few minutes later, Jenny dragged a kitchen chair out to the balcony and sat to feed the baby.

The sun was already heating the day. The square was quiet, only a jogger running nearby broke the stillness with the slap-slap of his shoes.

The fragrance of fresh coffee drifting across from the Café du Monde had her mouth watering. Since they had enjoyed Jared's first-day-back ritual yesterday, she suspected it would be up to her to prepare breakfast today. Not knowing what he liked, she'd bought a couple of boxes of cereal and some eggs yesterday. Or she could whip up some pancakes.

Toast and hot tea usually sufficed for her own breakfast. She knew that wouldn't be enough for a man Jared's size.

When Jamie finished eating, Jenny continued to hold her.

Maybe this afternoon she'd see about buying a few flowering plants. Since Jared didn't seem at all interested in keeping them after she left, she had to be judicious in her purchases. She'd have to take everything back to her apartment in Whitney—and her place wasn't large. Still, a few plants would be perfect and provide some needed color to the place.

"One down, two to go," Jared said from the doorway.

Jenny spun around. Her breath caught in her throat. He stood without the crutches, the walking cast obviously providing the freedom of movement he so wanted.

He should not look this yummy, she thought with a pang. His jeans were faded, ripped here and there, with one leg cut to allow for the cast. But they fit like a favorite old pair. Conscious of her gaze where it should not be, she forced it up. The loose cotton top he wore was a concession to the heat. The clinging cotton shirt revealed his muscular shoulders and arms.

"Meaning?" Jenny asked. Raising her gaze to meet his, she was struck again by the desire that engulfed her. He was sexy and dangerous and so appealing she hoped she could remember she was hired to watch the baby and not turn into a babbling idiot.

She couldn't help vividly remembering the feel of his body against hers last night, the brush of his breath across her cheeks, the tingling that shimmered when his hands threaded in her hair.

Oh, boy! She needed something to take her mind off the man. Couldn't she come up with some compelling reason to dislike him?

"It looks as if Jamie's eaten, so it's just you and me left to feed," he said easily. There was nothing in his manner to give a hint of the passion that had almost exploded between them last night. How did he turn it on and off?

"I suppose you like a big breakfast," Jenny said rising. She was relieved to note her knees worked. And he didn't appear to notice anything wrong. Thank goodness he couldn't read minds!

"Don't you?" he asked.

She shook her head. Would he move if she headed inside? Remembering his last comment—I still want a kiss—would he stop her and take up where they left off? She swallowed hard. Holding the baby upright against her shoulder, she licked her lips. Truth to tell, despite all the arguments she'd given herself last night, she wouldn't object if he kissed her.

Just once.

Or more than once.

"Did you buy eggs and bacon?" he asked.

She almost sighed. They were obviously not on the same wavelength.

"Eggs, no bacon. I can fix a cheese and mushroom omelet. And toast."

"Sounds good. Use at least three eggs for my portion. And a big pot of coffee."

"Okay." As she drew closer, she held out the baby like a shield. "Here, hold her. She's fed and burped and won't need a changing for a bit, I think. I can't watch her while I cook."

He gingerly took the baby beneath her arms and held her dubiously in front of him. "Where's her carrier?"

"Upstairs. I'll get it when we eat. You two can enjoy the morning quiet. The square will be bustling soon. Just hold her, Jared. She won't break."

She took a step to enter the living room, but Jared almost

stopped her in her tracks.

"Soon, Jenny," he promised, his eyes fixed on hers.

Flustered, she hurried into the kitchen and plunged into preparations. So much for thinking he'd forgotten their kiss. If she worked hard enough, maybe her pulse would slow to a normal rate.

Of course it would help if the fading bruises had marred his natural good looks. But they were hardly noticeable now. And it might help if he wore a suit and tie instead of showing off those muscular arms and the solid strength of his chest and all that tanned skin.

She almost laughed at her absurdity. The man was convalescing for heaven's sake. With a quiet groan, she forced herself to concentrate on preparing the omelet and ignoring every instinct that reminded her she was a woman.

The baby furniture was delivered shortly before noon. Jared had the deliverymen take everything except the rocking chair straight to Jenny's room.

"I was going to put her down for a nap," Jenny said as she watched the men disappear up the inside stairs. She could hear their heavy shoes on the floor above.

"Put her down in my room. We'll set everything up this afternoon and her bed will be ready by tonight," Jared suggested.

Jenny nodded. Entering his bedroom a minute later, she paused at the door. She'd explored the apartment when she'd first arrived, but Jared hadn't been home for months at that point. Every room had seemed impersonal. Now his stamp was clearly on every inch of his bedroom.

The covers on the king-size bed were tossed aside as if he'd just risen. She smiled. Obviously he wasn't one to think he had to make the bed immediately upon rising.

His suitcase lay opened on the floor—clothes still jumbled inside, a pair of jeans on the floor near the closet. His scent filled her.

"Lucky you, Jamie. You get to sleep in Jared's room for a while," Jenny said softly, crossing the room to the huge bed. She straightened the covers, moved pillows to make a barrier the infant couldn't breach. Then tucked her beneath a light blanket.

Jamie closed her eyes and in only a short time was fast asleep.

Jenny lay back on the bed beside her, gazing up at the ceiling. What would it be like to be part of a couple so in love they were in a world of their own? She'd thought she and Tad would marry, but she appreciated now that that was not a match made in heaven. For all she'd been hurt when she learned the truth behind his proposal, she also knew it would not have made her happy in the long run.

She wanted the passion she'd felt for a moment last night. She wanted to be totally enthralled with her husband. She wanted him totally enthralled with her. Imagine sharing all aspects of life together–eating meals together, sleeping together, and waking up together to face a new day. The bed was big and masculine, the covers dark and tailored. Nothing frilly about it. But she wouldn't mind sleeping in it—sharing it with its owner.

Startled, she rolled on her side and looked at the baby, then envisioned Jared lying beside her.

What kind of woman appealed to him? Blondes? Or was she just a convenient distraction while he couldn't get out and about?

There was nothing between them. She sighed, wishful thinking on her part.

Slowly she rose, feeling naive and inept. Since she and Tad were no longer engaged, she hated knowing she'd mistaken his attention as love.

It didn't matter, she tried to tell herself. But it taught her to be certain a man wanted her for herself alone and not as a partner to watch his children.

Walking to the door with one last glance at the baby, she shook her head. She was getting way ahead of herself. Jared said last night he wanted a kiss. Yet he'd made no move today to claim that kiss. Talk was cheap. Was he just teasing her? Wanting to see what she'd do?

Well, she'd do nothing. That would show him.

Sighing, she walked into her room to see what was going on. Jared had already ripped open one of the large cartons. It contained the dresser. No assembly there, at least.

"Where do you want this?" he asked.

Jenny looked up in surprise. "This is your place, where do you think?"

"I don't care. She's sharing the room with you, not me. You decide."

"Then against that wall. Her crib can be there and we'll move my bed over near the window," Jenny said, pointing out spots in the room.

In no time, despite the cast, Jared had rearranged her bed and dresser, placed Jamie's new dresser in the spot indicated and was starting to open the box containing the crib.

"Need any help?" Jenny asked, keeping a healthy distance from him. She was fixated on that kiss yet refused to let Jared know.

If he wanted to kiss her, he could make the first move.

"Yes, when we assemble it, you hold it while I set the fasteners."

Jenny followed his instructions willingly. It was an easy assembly and in no time he was tightening the last screw. He glanced up at her.

"Now you have experience for when you marry that paragon you're looking for and have your own family."

"Experience?"

"Setting up a nursery. You can tell your husband how you learned everything down in New Orleans one summer."

"Umm, maybe," she said doubtfully.

He raised an eyebrow. "Only maybe?"

"Depends on what all I learn this summer," she said daringly.

"And what all do you want to learn, Jenny?" He stood up, gazing at her intently. His eyes were no longer teasing. For a moment Jenny felt as if the two of them were alone in the world. That they were a part of each other, building a life together.

What would it take to convince Jared being part of a family wasn't so terrible? That building a future together could be a wonderful part of life? That he might even enjoy it?

She blinked as sanity returned. She wasn't here to change his mind about anything. Just to care for Jamie.

"Nothing you can teach me," she said slowly. "Unless it's more about drilling for oil."

He held her gaze for another moment, then looked away. Was that disappointment she saw? Wishful thinking on her part, more likely.

Quickly moving to put some distance between them, she

began picking up the cardboard and bending and crushing it into manageable sizes.

"Tell me where to put this and I'll take it down."

He gave her directions to the trash area and handed her several folded pieces. She almost tripped in her haste to leave. Maybe a few minutes alone would let her gain a semblance of sense and stop the steamy images that constantly played in her mind whenever she was near Jared. Or thought about him.

Jared listened to her rush down the stairs and sank back on the floor, leaning against the wall. He stretched his legs out in front of him and rested his head against the cool plaster wall. Last night he blamed the pain pills for his coming on so strong.

Now that he hadn't touched her once all day he wondered if he could still sidestep around the real reason.

He had the hots for his pretty nanny, there was no denying that.

At least today he seemed better able to control his urges. He thought last night she was interested—interested enough to be a willing participant. Until they were interrupted and she'd taken off like a cat with a scalded tail. Now he didn't know what to think.

She watched him warily. No denying that. Had he been out of the dating game so long he couldn't even read the signs anymore?

No, no one was out that long!

Is there anything else you want to learn this summer? Loaded with innuendo and she hadn't missed it a mite. Jenny wasn't the type to jump into bed with a near stranger, no matter how much he wished she was—just this one time.

She was lace curtains, monogamous relationships, kids and puppies and PTA meetings. It wouldn't be fair to attempt to talk her into anything different. She was helping him by taking care of Jamie. If he didn't watch himself, he'd send her running in the opposite direction leaving him alone with a baby and full of regrets.

Rubbing his palm over his face, he looked around the room. It was crowded with the baby furniture— but only temporarily. Soon he'd call his attorney and start the proceedings that would find Jamie a nice home. He wasn't sure how long it would take, but he had weeks before he'd be back in shape to return to work.

And he had to deal with his parents.

And the growing attraction for Jenny.

At the moment, he wasn't sure which would be easier.

Getting awkwardly to his feet, he was glad she wasn't there to see him.

He wondered how long it would be before he was back in shape. Moving gingerly to make sure he didn't jar anything, he gathered up the rest of the trash from the packaging. He'd carry it down to the main floor and let Jenny take it out.

Then he'd review the preliminary reports about the explosion once more—see if he could pinpoint what had gone wrong and what they could do to insure such an event never happened again. Not for the first time, he wished Jim was there. He had an uncanny eye for problem areas. What had happened this time?

He stopped in the doorway and glanced over his shoulder. Already the guest room looked foreign. Having a woman and baby around the place did that. The crib was made up with colorful sheets and bumper pads depicting Winnie-the-Pooh. A mobile moved gently in the stirring air. Stacks of diapers had already been put away in the dresser. The pad on top would cushion the baby while she was being changed.

How many more changes would these two females bring before they were gone?

Any change would be temporary. Once Jamie was taken care of, once his cast was off and the doctor declared him fit, he was leaving. Once back in the middle east it might be another two years, or longer, before he returned to New Orleans.

By then, Jenny would probably be married with a baby of her own.

Stomping down the stairs, Jared tried to ignore the disquiet that thought produced. Tried to ignore the fact that he wasn't as excited about resuming work as he should be. And it wasn't all due to the injuries that still hadn't healed. It was a restlessness that had his thoughts in turmoil and his emotions rocking.

Living in the Middle East wouldn't be the same with Jim gone. They'd been friends since second grade. Jared had attended the funeral for Jim's mother when she'd died while they'd been in their teens. And returned for the one for Jim's father five years ago.

Jim had been there for him when he decided he couldn't stay with Andrea and had urged him to apply for foreign assignments. Then joined him, despite being married.

Margaret and his children still lived in Whitney. Which was the primary reason he had no intention of visiting at all. It was too soon to face their grief on top of his own. Knowing Jim had betrayed her made it all the more difficult.

Which pointed out yet another reason to avoid marriage. If Jim and Margaret couldn't make it, what chance did he have?

Jenny's comments about no one caring for him rankled. He

had plenty of people who cared for him. He had his life just like he wanted it.

Jared deposited the cardboard near the door and lifted the rocker and carried it carefully to the balcony. His ankle ached. He sat down and stared over Jackson Square, his mind several thousand miles away reliving the explosion, the fire, the chaos that reigned when everyone had been caught unaware by the unexpected eruption.

Suddenly he felt tired beyond belief. Drained. Leaning back, he closed his eyes and willed his mind to empty of the horrifying images, and the knowledge that his best friend was gone forever.

He had other friends. He just had to reestablish contact. But not today.

Chapter Twelve

Two days later Jared again sat in the rocker. This time he was holding Jamie. For someone who hadn't wanted anything to do with the baby, he sure spent a lot of time holding her. Every time he turned around, it seemed, Jenny thrust the baby into his arms. Always with some excuse—mainly that Jamie needed to be held. He thought that's why they'd invented infant carriers.

Jamie gazed solemnly up at him as he slowly rocked. What did babies think about, he wondered? Was she curious who he was? Who Jenny was? Did she miss her mother? Jim?

When her gaze moved to fix on the colorful red flowers cascading down the side of a hanging basket he smiled. She was attracted to the bold colors just as Jenny had predicted. He let his own gaze roam the balcony.

It looked like a florist shop. He recognized the daisies and the marigolds, but none of the other flowers. He bet his mother would know instantly what each variety was.

She liked gardens. They were her passion—just as longing to travel seemed to be his father's.

He remembered Jenny's caustic comment that first day, and then wondered for the first time how his mother did feel listening to his father's constant complaining about being stuck in Whitney because of her, because of their early marriage. How had she put up with it and him, for all those years?

"I brought you some iced tea. Are you sure you don't mind having Mrs. Giraux over for dinner? She's alone so much, I thought this would be a nice change for her."

Jenny stepped onto the small balcony and handed him a frosty glass. She had a bottle of cool water for Jamie. Holding it out to him, she looked at him with a quizzical expression.

"When you asked yesterday, I said I didn't mind. You asked again before you invited her this morning. Isn't it a bit late for me to change my mind now? She'll be here in a few minutes," he said, drinking deeply, then setting the glass down and reaching for the baby bottle.

He was getting good at this—not that anyone needed to know that.

"Umm, yes, but you don't seem at all enthusiastic about it."

"Jenny, she's in her seventies. What do we have in common?"

She shrugged and looked troubled. He wanted to brush that frown from her forehead, tell her she'd get wrinkles, tease her into laughing. Instead he looked at Jamie and kept his hands to himself.

Over the last couple of days, he'd stayed as far away from Jenny as he could. They ate meals together since he hadn't figured out how to go without eating. Jenny was a good cook; he'd missed home cooking. But he'd tried to keep their conversation on a superficial level. When that didn't work, Jenny talked about Jamie.

Once he'd asked her about her career, but found it hard to relate to stories of children when he'd been away from them for so long. Most men at the foreign sites left their families

Stateside. Or were single to begin with. The high pay made separations acceptable.

In fact, when he thought about it, he wasn't around women that much either. Did they all have this nesting instinct?

Jenny had added enough flowers to fill a good-size yard, much less a small balcony. Inside she'd also made changes. Two colorful braided rugs in the living room, bunches of flowers in vases, a pastel blue Monet print on the wall. Soft decorative pillows on the sofa.

He waited for the usual sense of claustrophobia to take hold. It hadn't as of yet, which surprised him.

Whenever he thought of Andrea and the way she'd insisted on decorating every room with more things in it than he could stand, he'd almost break out into a sweat.

But the few changes Jenny had made he could live with. In fact, though he wouldn't want to tell her for fear of encouraging her to do even more, he liked it. The colors were soothing, yet brightened the room.

The changes made the apartment feel—welcoming.

He frowned. Now he was imagining things. An apartment was an apartment, and allowing Jenny to add a few colorful knickknacks changed nothing.

He stood abruptly. The last thing he needed was to get complaisant about some fancy decorated rooms. His apartment in the United Arab Emirates was spartan and he liked it that way. He traveled fastest who traveled light.

"I've got work to do," he said, holding out the baby for her to take.

"You aren't going to disappear into your bedroom when Mrs. Giraux arrives, are you?" Jenny asked, clearly disappointed as she reached to take Jamie. "She's coming to visit with both of us. I know she misses her husband."

"So I'm the token male at the table?"

Jenny smiled and shrugged. "If the shoe fits. Oh, she's getting bigger, don't you think?" she asked when she took the baby's full weight. "I'm sure she weighs more than she did when I first saw her. When are we taking her to the doctor's?"

"Is she sick?" Jared asked. Jamie seemed fine to him.

"Of course not, but babies need to see a doctor every few weeks, to get their immunizations, and make sure they are growing and all. He'll tell us when to start solid foods, what to look for as she grows."

"Her new parents can locate a doctor. That'll be time enough," he said, snagging his glass and stepping inside.

Jenny kissed Jamie's head and looked after Jared. "Did you call your attorney yet?"

"I'll get to it tomorrow. If you think she needs a doctor before then, call someone."

"I don't know any here in New Orleans," she said, stepping inside. After the brightness of the balcony, it took a few seconds for her eyes to adjust.

Jared stood beside her. "Ask Mrs. Giraux, I bet she'll know a few."

"Pediatricians?"

He shrugged. "If not, I'll bet she can find out in short order. She's lived here her entire life, she must know a lot of people."

"Then why doesn't she have more friends over?"

Jared cupped her chin and raised her face. "Ask her that tonight. Maybe she's a hermit in disguise."

Jenny caught her breath. She should be getting used to this.

Jared had touched her frequently over the last couple of days, brushing his fingers against hers if she handed him something. Bumping into her in the tight space of the kitchen. Each time she felt the contact to her toes. She stepped back, dislodging his hand. Color flew to her cheeks. Jared gave a half smile and headed for the stairs.

"There's more to this baby business than I want to deal with," he said. "I'd rather have geological puzzles any day."

"It's not that complex," Jenny mumbled, torn with wanting him to leave and wishing he'd stay.

Shaking her head, she headed for the kitchen to check on her seafood casserole. She wanted dinner to be especially nice for their neighbor. Concentrate on that, she admonished herself, not her infuriating boss! At least Mrs. Giraux would act as a buffer during dinner. Which bought Jenny some time to get her emotions under some kind of control.

She frowned. So far she wasn't doing so well in that.

"Thank you for inviting me for dinner," Mrs. Giraux said when she entered the apartment late that afternoon. She handed Jenny a plate of pralines. "I hope you can find a use for these. The recipe's from my late mother-in-law. Samuel and I always liked pralines."

"Thank you. I love them and bet Jared does, too. Do you think we could break off a bit without the nuts and let Jamie taste?"

"Oh, dear, I'm not sure about that."

"See, something to ask the doctor," Jenny said over her shoulder to Jared.

"The doctor?" Mrs. Giraux asked.

"Umm, I was telling Jared we should find a pediatrician for Jamie. He thinks it can wait, but this is just the kind of thing we could ask. And I don't know where she stands with immunizations."

"I think the baby can live a little longer without any pralines," he said, sitting stiffly in the easy chair opposite the sofa.

"He thinks we should wait and let her new parents find a pediatrician." One thing Jenny had learned at the children's home was to deal with the truth, no matter how painful.

Mrs. Giraux studied her with a twinkle in her eye. "You said before that the baby was going to a different home, but I chose to disbelieve it. I can't have my favorite baby whisked away from me, now can I?" she asked, smiling at Jamie's solemn gaze.

Propped up in the baby carrier, Jamie wore a ruffled pink dress Jenny had bought on their shopping spree. A matching ribbon adorned her curly black hair. Jenny had adored dressing up little girls when they were at the Home. Much more fun than little boys. Of course, boys had their own charm, with their determination to achieve whatever they set their minds on.

Unexpectedly, she missed Tad's sons. They'd done a lot together over the winter months and she had come to love those little boys. If only their father could have loved her for who she was and not merely sought to obtain a permanent live-in nanny.

"Care for some sherry?" Jenny asked their guest. "I bought some yesterday. You don't have much of a bar," she said wrinkling her nose at Jared.

"No point in stocking too much, I'm never here for long."

"That's true. In the eight years you've rented this place, I bet you have never stayed a full month at one time," Mrs. Giraux said.

"Really?" Jenny asked, carrying a glass to each of them. "Why keep an apartment if you aren't going to use it?"

"I use it, just not a lot. I get mail sent here."

Jared studied the three females opposite him. Did they purposely sit together on the wide sofa? Mrs. Giraux represented the Old South, Jenny would exemplify the new. What would life hold for Jamie?

"Can't be very important mail if you don't get home to read it except every couple of years," Jenny murmured.

"I for one am glad things have changed for the time being. It's nice to have neighbors. Sometimes I worry about falling or something and when there's no one in the adjacent apartment, I could have been stuck for days before getting help," Mrs. Giraux said brightly.

"Nothing's changed. As soon as my leg is healed, I'm heading back," Jared said sharply. He looked at Jenny—had she led his neighbor to suspect something different?

"Oh, with Jamie and all, I thought for sure you'd choose to work closer to home. She'll need you as she grows up, you know."

"Jared doesn't think anyone needs him. And he's sure he needs no one to depend on him!" Jenny said, her challenging gaze meeting his.

"Nonsense, everyone needs someone," Mrs. Giraux said firmly.

"Some people think their lives aren't complete if they don't have a family surrounding them," Jared drawled, daring Jenny to comment with that lopsided smile of his. "Others like to keep moving. There's a lot of world out there to explore."

Jenny hated his mocking tone! There was nothing wrong in wishing for a family. He'd realize that if he didn't already have roots. If he didn't already know where he came from. If he didn't have parents and a sister and nephews.

"At least I'd appreciate my family if I had one. I'd want to be around them, and do things together. Build memories. Not ignore them for years on end!" she retorted.

"I have memories. Maybe mine aren't as pleasant as the fairy-tale ones you're dreaming about. Not every family's perfect. Only the ones in dreams or TV sitcoms."

"I never said anything about a perfect family. But learning to get along is part of the process. It's not all one sided."

"Am I missing some part of this conversation?" Mrs. Giraux asked, looking from one to the other in bewilderment.

Jenny shook her head and tried to calm down. Why did Jared's comments drive her crazy? They didn't agree on what they each found important, she knew that, yet she continued to try to change his mind.

It wasn't going to happen. He'd had years to grow into the man he was. His philosophy of life was ingrained and her idealistic dreams of a family weren't going to change his beliefs.

Why take it personally? Once her job was finished, she'd never have to see him again.

"Sorry, Mrs. G. It seems Jared and I have different opinions about families and somehow just keep arguing about what's important. Which I certainly shouldn't be doing since he pays my wages this summer. Arguing with the boss isn't a great idea."

"I'm buying your baby-sitting services, not paying you to be a yes-man," he said quickly.

"So nice to hear that." She smiled sweetly, knowing he'd recognize it as false.

'Families are important. Jamie will need a lot of love and attention over the years. Not every man can take on the responsibilities of another man's child," Mrs. Giraux said slowly, her gaze on the baby. "Samuel couldn't. I so longed for children. When we couldn't have them, I wanted to adopt a baby. He refused."

Jenny's heart ached for her new friend. She knew how much Mrs. Giraux must have longed for a baby. To never have one must be a sad thing to live with.

Mrs. Giraux looked at Jenny. "It was the only thing he really refused me, so I shouldn't complain."

"I'm sorry," Jenny said gently.

"Oh, I got over it long ago. We had a happy life together. But it's lonely now that there's just me. If we'd had children, maybe we would have had grandchildren as well. Someone to share holidays with, to remember my birthday."

She looked up and shook her head. "Listen to me, I'm almost maudlin. Pay me no mind. I sound like an old woman!"

"Think of Jamie as your granddaughter while she's here," Jenny suggested softly.

"She's not staying, so don't go getting attached!" Jared snapped. He rose and glared at them. "I should have called my attorney already. First thing tomorrow I'm getting on the phone to start the ball rolling."

With that, he walked out to the balcony. Resting his palms on the railing, he stared out over the square.

"Oh dear, I didn't mean to upset him," Mrs. Giraux said.

Jamie gurgled and kicked her feet, drawing the woman's attention.

Jenny smiled at the baby, then the smile faded as she stared after Jared. "You know, Mrs. Giraux, I've been here five days now and he's yet to make that phone call. I just realized it."

"Now isn't that interesting?"

"Maybe. Want to hold the baby?"

Chapter Thirteen

Jared tightened his grip on the railing. He could hear the soft murmur of feminine voices behind him, but he ignored them. Anger roiled inside. He'd handled the entire situation wrong. He should have left Jamie in the U.A.E. Or he should have gone straight to Whitney and turned her over to the children's home. Why hadn't he thought of that? The orphanage would have taken good care of her. They'd have looked for a suitable home.

Suddenly the image of Jim and Sohany at their small apartment rose. They'd been so delighted with their little girl. The love they'd shared changed Jim, made him easier to deal with, less restless. And for a fourth baby, Jim seemed besotted with the child.

It was understandable. Jamie was cute. Small, but he expected the American diet to soon remedy that. Jim had been a tall man, maybe she'd take after him, though her eyes were dark like Sohany's. Would she favor either parent, or be a blend of them both?

He might never know. Once she had her new parents, he needn't stay involved. Wouldn't it just confuse a child to have him pop into her life from time to time? The adoptive parents would probably want no reminders of her past.

You are the link to her parents, Jenny'd said.

Like it made him special.

Maybe he could write down all he knew about Jamie's parents and send it with her when she found a home. Jenny had jotted some notes, he could take those and expand them. Write a biography for Jamie to read when she was older.

Great, that would take time. He should be making arrangements immediately. He could send his notes later.

Or could he?

Maybe he'd wait another day or two before calling Arthur and jot down what he remembered. See about finding those photographs Jenny suggested before time and distance made it difficult.

"Jared?" Jenny stepped out on the balcony, Jamie held in her arms.

"What?" He turned and leaned against the only spot on the railing not filled with flowers. Looking at her he was struck by the uncertainty in her gaze. She smiled tentatively and held the baby up toward him.

"I'm going to put her down now, I thought you'd want to say good-night."

He clenched his hands into fists. Since their trip to purchase furniture, she'd insisted he act as a substitute for Jamie's father. The designated daddy. Despite his telling her he didn't want to become involved, it was hard to resist.

The baby scent of talc and milk seemed familiar now. He didn't want to grow to know the baby, develop feelings for her. All babies were cute, whether human, dogs or cats. Even baby camels had an innocent beguiling look to them. It didn't mean he needed to grow attached.

"She doesn't care," he said.

"You don't know that. I bet she loves to be told good-night by everyone around."

Jenny stepped closer tilting the baby toward him. He could smell the talc again, and the fragrance of the flowers on the balcony and Jenny's special scent, light and sweet.

The baby was close. Jenny was close. He could brush a kiss on Jamie's cheek, move a few inches and capture Jenny's lips. He fantasized about kissing her at night.

Or sometimes when he was trying to decipher the reports he received from work.

Or when she gave him some smart answer to a question.

Heck, he fantasized about kissing her all the time.

It was dumb. He didn't need any involvement with her any more than he needed to become attached to this baby.

But he knew tenacity when he saw it.

He almost gave in to the urge to brush his lips across hers.

"Good night, Jamie," he said softly, his eyes on Jenny's tempting mouth.

"Dinner will be on the table in ten minutes," she said, turning swiftly and heading inside.

Had she felt the stirring of desire? Color rose in her cheeks, but it could be from the heat.

Jared preferred to think she was as aware of him as he was of her. One of these days he'd forget his intentions, forget she was his employee for the summer and kiss her silly.

Turning, he frowned. He was becoming fixated on Jenny Stratford. Proximity, that was all it was. That and his weakness for blondes—especially one with pretty blue eyes, who found enchantment in everything around her.

He needed to get out and spend some time with other people. For a moment, he wondered who he could call. His visits to New Orleans were too infrequent to keep in close contact with anyone. There'd been a few women he dated from time to time. But two years was a long gap and he didn't want to just call up anybody and ask her out.

What he wanted to do was to ask Jenny out.

Gripping the balcony again he forced that idea away. He'd call some of the men he knew at the home office. Surely they'd be up for a beer after work or a night on the town. All he had to do was get through dinner tonight, then make it clear to Jenny that she was paid to watch the baby, nothing more.

She'd already made changes in the apartment, with the flowers and the baby furniture and the new picture she'd picked up from one of the sidewalk artists yesterday. Leaning against the sofa, he suspected it wouldn't be long before she'd hang it like she had the Monet—offering another colorful addition to the plain walls.

Nesting instincts were fine for those who wanted to build a home. He was leaving as soon as his leg healed. His home right now was in the U.A.E.

At least for the next several months.

After that he didn't know where he'd be sent.

Dinner had been a disaster, Jenny thought as she wiped the last of the dishes. Mrs. Giraux had been pleasant, but left as soon as the cherry cobbler had been consumed. Her nervous glances at Jared could be excused—Jared had been distant, silent, bordering on rude—almost as if he regretted letting Jenny invite his neighbor.

She wanted to smack him for his rudeness. Their neighbor had enjoyed getting out. It wouldn't hurt to show some kindness.

As soon as Mrs. Giraux left, he'd gone to his room. The sound when he slammed the door was like a shot. She listened intensely for a few minutes, afraid he'd wakened Jamie.

So much for trying to build relationships between neighbors, she thought wryly as she stacked the plates in the cupboard. It had been as much for Jared as Mrs. Giraux. She'd never met a man as alone as he. Surely everyone needed friends or at least neighbors they could count on.

The problem came when the talk turned to the baby, she thought He'd been cordial until Mrs. Giraux had urged him to raise his friend's child. He'd been mad she's shared that information with Mrs. G.

Then Jenny hadn't helped matters when she offered to let Jamie consider herself as a grandchild to Mrs. Giraux. As if they'd have a future together. But the woman was lonely and it wouldn't hurt to let her spend some time with the baby. She adored Jamie and it gave her something to look forward to. How could he not see that?

The thought constantly nagged—if he gave Jamie up, one day he'd regret it.

Or was that just wishful thinking on her part? She'd never give her up if she was hers. But she wasn't a man. Or Jared.

He never let himself soften an inch. He held Jamie, brushed his lips across her cheek once in a while when he thought Jenny couldn't see, but he didn't really play with her, or talk to her or ever ask to hold her.

Just once, Jenny wished he'd volunteer to take the baby while she drank her bottle or became fretful. It made her heart ache to think of Jamie with no parents, no family, no history.

"It's not your business!" she repeated firmly as she

dropped the forks and knives in the slots in the drawer. "Don't go falling for this baby just because she loves to snuggle up with you or her eyes are so alert she seems to really understand you when you talk!"

And especially don't fall for her reluctant daddy, Jenny admonished herself silently.

Was that advice coming too late?

On the balcony, earlier she'd yearned to feel Jared's lips on hers. And not a simple sweep across the cheek like he sometimes gave Jamie. If only the phone had not rung the other night! Would she have found pulsating pleasure in his kisses?

Yet a kiss would mean little beyond a brief pleasure. He had nothing to offer a woman like her. A more determined man she'd never met.

And he was determined to go through life alone.

"Dinner was good," Jared said from the doorway, a guarded look in his expression.

Jenny spun around, grateful she'd not been talking to herself. When had he come back downstairs? She hadn't heard him.

"I appreciate your letting me invite Mrs. Giraux over. I enjoyed her visit. Her stories of growing up in New Orleans are fascinating. And how she survived Katrina. And the changes to the Garden District over the years." Jenny didn't know a lot about New Orleans and could listen to Mrs. Giraux for hours.

"Invite her anytime you want, but in the future, don't include me," he said.

"You don't like her?"

"That has nothing to do with liking her. She's nice enough. Reminds me of my grandmother. I told you that. I don't want to raise expectations that can't be met. I'm sorry she doesn't have a next door neighbor who comes home every night, that would love to listen to her tales of New Orleans when she was young, that would be around if she falls, or needs some assistance. But I'm not that neighbor. I'll be gone again in a few weeks and won't be back for months."

"I enjoy her stories," Jenny said defensively, holding on tightly to the damp dish towel.

"I did, too." He rested a shoulder against the door- jamb and crossed his arms across his chest. "I said you could invite her over."

"Just don't include you. Right, I got the message. I just don't understand it. What are you planning to do if I invite her over, eat in your room? Don't you want company sometimes? People to laugh with or make memories?"

He shook his head, his gaze studying her as if she were an alien creature. "Jenny Stratford, you are one romantic woman. You want fairy-tale stories with happy endings for everything. But you have nothing on Mrs. Giraux. Look at her apartment, look at the feminine lacy dresses she wears. Look at the stars in her eyes when she looks at you and me. She's hearing wedding bells."

Jenny turned, feeling hurt at the mocking tone of his voice. She spread the towel to dry and then wished she'd kept it. She had nothing to do now but leave the kitchen and didn't know how she could do so with Jared blocking the door.

"You made it perfectly clear that any other ties or relationships are not in your future. I'm sure she got the message."

"Did you?" he asked softly.

She spun around at that. Hands on hips, she was glad for

the spurt of anger that swept through her.

"I got that message day one. Don't worry about me. You're not my idea of husband material. I want someone who wants to be home every night; who wants lots of children, a picket fence, a dog and camping vacations and the PTA and everything! You're not even on the track, much less in the running."

"Just so we're clear on that" he said, pushing away from the doorjamb and walking across the kitchen floor. His walking cast made an odd thump while his other leg was silent.

"What are you doing?" she asked, backing up against the counter. He drew relentlessly closer.

"Finally collecting on my good-night kiss," he said reaching out to enclose her in his arms.

Jenny had no time to protest—even if she wanted to, which she wasn't sure she did.

She'd been aching to feel his mouth on hers, to have those strong hands cradle her head again, to feel the passion that seemed to shimmer around him.

She closed her eyes and waited.

Once again he threaded his fingers in her soft hair, tilted up her head and leaned closer. She could feel his breath caress her face.

"Only one kiss and no more," Jared said.

With that, he ended the waiting.

Chapter Fourteen

His lips were warm and firm, moving so sensuously across her own she wondered if she could remain standing. She felt a lovely, lethargic weakness sweep through her. His hands held her head for his kiss and she shivered at the shimmering waves of delight that skimmed across her. When he nudged her lips, she parted them, allowing him full access to her mouth.

Swept away, like the rush of tidewater at flood stage in the Mississippi.

It was glorious.

She moved to get closer as if she could meld her body into his. Awareness narrowed from the world around them to the narrow confines of the two of them locked together in a fiery embrace that went on and on.

Heat built—and demanded. Passion matched passion and still she yearned for more. She stretched up to encircle his neck with her arms, to draw him closer still, holding on tightly. Reveling in the sweet sensations that cascaded.

Did it last for a minute or a lifetime? Jenny wasn't sure. She lost track of time—floating on the sensual bliss of his magical kiss.

He demanded a response which she gave freely. Heat continued to build even as her breath was lost. But she didn't need to breathe. What she had needed all her life was now in her arms.

When he eased back, she didn't want to let go. Her arms tightened their hold, but he wasn't leaving, only turning slightly to kiss her cheeks, rain caresses across her face. When he caught his breath, his mouth moved to hers again. Blood thundered in her ears, blotting out all other sounds. She craved his touch, his mouth, his lips. How had she lived this long without them?

Long minutes later Jared pulled back, resting his forehead on hers, gazing down into her eyes when she slowly raised her lids. Why had he stopped?

"You're dangerous, you know that, don't you?" he said in a husky voice. "We stop now. Unless you say we go on."

Jenny blinked. Reality returned in an instant.

She dropped her arms, resting her hands against his biceps. The kitchen was hot, she was hot, yet the dread that suddenly sprang up chilled her.

She was not ready for anything else. Not with Jared.

Licking her lips, she took a deep breath. She felt surrounded by his scent. His body still pressed hers against the counter.

Jared Montgomery had made his position crystal clear. An affair would be all he'd want.

Jenny knew she could never agree to something like that.

Already she felt an attraction that was dangerously like falling in love. She was more aware and attuned to him than she'd ever been to Tad—or any other man.

But she wasn't one to give into impulse, nor hop into bed with anyone who stirred her senses. A kiss was as far as she knew she could go.

Jared hesitated a moment, then stepped back. His gaze never left hers.

"You make the next move. You let me know, okay?" he said, his voice husky.

She nodded, then slipped around to the side and ran for the stairs. In seconds she was in her room, leaning against the door breathing as hard as if she'd run a race. She almost laughed at her melodramatic reaction.

He hadn't pursued her.

He was going to let her set the boundaries.

Then she almost cried. After that kiss, they should be seeing what each could mean for the other. Instead, there would be boundaries. And limits and a definite end when Jamie was gone and Jared's leg healed.

Jenny pressed her palms against her cheeks, feeling the heat that probably had them red as poppies. Closing her eyes, she remembered vividly every second of that fiery, explosive kiss.

"Who would expect a kiss between strangers to be so startling," she whispered into the night. "So complete, yet unfinished."

It was nothing like an end-of-date kiss with other men she'd gone out with over the years.

And that scared her. Scared her and thrilled her and had her wondering if she dare try it one more time.

Just once more.

When Jenny brought Jamie downstairs the next morning, the living room was empty. It was still early, but most mornings Jared had already had the coffee on and was reading the interminable reports his printer seemed to spit out with great regularity.

Thankful that he hadn't made an appearance yet this morning, she prepared Jamie's bottle and took her out into the cool morning air. She sat in the rocker and tried to remember all the opening gambits she'd rehearsed last night for when she next saw Jared. She'd be friendly, cordial. But cool.

Definitely in control. That was a must.

Jared had probably had dozens of affairs over the years.

She wished she could pretend she'd done the same. She didn't want him laughing at her or feeling sorry for her. She was going to be logical.

Didn't men relish logic?

If he brought up the subject, she'd say she wasn't looking for an affair. She'd do her job and leave when the time came with no complications. They had nothing in common and it would make more sense to keep their personal lives separate. She hoped she could pull it off. If he gave her that lopsided smile, her insides would melt and she'd be tempted to throw caution to the wind and see what developed.

She gazed at Jamie. "You're lucky. For now you only have to worry about getting fed and bathed and changed. And I'll take good care of you. Wait until you grow up and face all the problems that are thrown at you." Cuddling her closer, she smiled at the infant, wishing for a moment when she, too, would have no worries beyond when to eat or when to bathe.

Jamie watched her from her dark eyes, never letting her gaze stray.

"You're filling out a bit, I think, sweetie. You look like you've gained a little weight. We need to find a doctor and see how big you are."

Jenny relished the closeness of the baby, the utter trust Jamie placed in her to take care of her needs. She was close to falling so in love with this little girl she would be crushed when they had to part.

Jenny pushed the thought away. She'd known coming into the job that any relationship with the baby was strictly temporary. Instead, she tried to ignore the coming separation and focused her attention on how she would prepare her classroom for the fall, the things she needed to do before school started. But between enjoying Jamie and listening for Jared, she couldn't hold a single thought of the future. She was too much a part of the present.

Long after the baby finished eating, Jenny continued to rock her. She'd start breakfast when she heard Jared. Now, she was content to avoid their first meeting.

She held Jamie up and carried her around the balcony so she could see each flower. Tickling her cheeks with the soft blossoms, she laughed when the baby batted them with her flailing hands. The bright reds and pinks caught the baby's attention and she'd try to reach for them.

"One day your eye-hand coordination will work," Jenny said with a soft giggle. Then she snatched Jamie close and kissed her cheek. "And where will you be then, I wonder?"

"With parents who love her," Jared said from the doorway.

Jenny took a deep breath, tried to quell the butterflies that suddenly danced in her stomach. Turning, she smiled brightly, holding the baby as a shield. She'd get through this awkward morning-after.

"She's eaten. I can fix our breakfast now if you like. Do you want to hold her while I do?"

He seemed to hesitate, his eyes searching hers. Then he

shrugged and held out his hands. "Why not? I'm becoming a pro at this."

His fingers brushed against hers when she handed him Jamie. For a second, Jenny's breath caught. Then she stepped around him and hurried into the kitchen, glad for a chance to be alone. She hoped she had put last night's kiss in perspective. They were two single people, attracted slightly to each other. A kiss was not the end of the world.

As she prepared hot cakes and sausage patties, Jenny forced herself to plan a busy day. She'd take the baby for a long walk and explore more of the French Quarter. Maybe the two of them could have lunch at that sidewalk café on Royal Street. This afternoon while Jamie napped, she'd see about locating a pediatrician and scheduling an appointment. Even if Jared followed through and contacted his attorney today, Jamie needed to see a doctor soon. And adoptions took some time, didn't they? Jenny wanted the best care possible as long as she was in charge of the baby.

Jared walked into the kitchen with Jamie just as Jenny was pouring fresh orange juice in their glasses. The coffee was hot, its fragrance filling the room. She smiled brightly, avoiding his eyes, and settled the baby in her infant seat. Once again her hands tangled with his.

Accidentally, or deliberately?

She ignored the sensations that his touch engendered and quickly began to serve the meal.

Jared brought some papers which he began to read, obviously not wanting conversation at the table. That suited Jenny. She ate, watched the baby and every once in a while darted a glance at Jared while she tried to forget that kiss.

He looked up at one point and met her gaze, his giving

nothing away.

"I won't be home for dinner tonight," Jared said as he rose. He filled his mug with coffee and stacked the papers.

"Oh? Okay, thanks for letting me know," she said, amazed at the intense disappointment that hit her. She dropped her gaze to her coffee cup. Was he going on a date? Since she had not thrown herself into his arms last night, was he now looking for feminine companionship elsewhere?

He looked at her sharply. "Are you all right?"

She nodded, hoping he could not detect the disappointment

"Of course! You don't need to baby-sit me, Jared. I'll take care of Jamie as I'm paid to do. We'll manage perfectly. Maybe go exploring a bit today. If I don't have to fix dinner, we can stay out longer."

"Don't stay out beyond dark. The Quarter gets a bit rowdy then."

She nodded, hoping he'd leave before the smile cracked her face.

He'd hired her to watch Jamie. Nothing more. There was no reason to feel hurt he was taking someone else out. To know he'd prefer the company of another woman to hers. If she thought about it, he'd offered her first chance. It was her own fault she hadn't followed through with the invitation.

Jenny cleaned the kitchen in record time. Taking Jamie up to bathe and dress, she couldn't wait to leave for their sightseeing venture. She'd explore every bit of New Orleans over the next few days. This might be her only time to have an all-expenses-paid visit— so it was up to her to take advantage of it.

Jared was on the phone when she came down with the

baby. She hesitated a moment as she placed Jamie in the baby carrier. Who was he calling so early? The attorney? Or the woman he was taking out that night?

The attorney most likely. He must have already made arrangements for the evening before coming to breakfast.

Tears gathered in the back of her throat. She rushed through the living room gathering the things she wanted. Lifting the stroller, she headed outside. A few minutes later she had carried everything down except the baby. Returning one last time to the apartment, Jenny picked up Jamie, trying to eavesdrop without appearing to.

But Jared's comments were limited to yeses and nos. And a final, "...fine, I'll see you then."

None of which gave her a clue to the full conversation.

By the time Jenny returned to the apartment in the late afternoon, she was hot, slightly sunburned and so tired she felt she could sleep a week. She'd deliberately stayed away in hopes of getting her thoughts and emotions under control.

Pushing the stroller all day, she'd tried to think about Jamie and the fun they were having. But the knowledge that Jared had started proceedings to send the baby away weighed heavily on her mind.

As did the thought of his date.

She couldn't stand to return home before he'd left for dinner. What if he asked her how he looked when he was on his way out?

Did men do that? she wondered, then brushed the thought aside. It didn't matter. She had no intention of seeing him dressed up to take someone else out and pretend she didn't care.

She did care. She was jealous that he wanted to spend time with someone else.

Mrs. Giraux peeked out of her apartment as Jenny was struggling to bring up the stroller, the purchases she'd made and the diaper bag all in one trip. She'd already taken Jamie into the apartment and didn't want to keep running up and down the stairs.

"Hello," Mrs. Giraux called. "Do you need help?"

"Hi, Mrs. G. No, I think I can manage. The door's open, pop in and check on Jamie. I'll be up in two secs."

"I don't want to interrupt Jared," the older woman said.

"You're not. Jared's not home, if you're worrying about that. And I'm always glad for your company."

By the time Jenny entered the apartment and set down the stroller and the bags, Mrs. Giraux had picked Jamie up and was holding her, though the baby was fast asleep.

"She'll wake up before bedtime, but I bet she'll sleep well tonight We did so much today, I bet she's exhausted. I know I am," Jenny said as she plopped down on the sofa and leaned her head back. Closing her eyes felt so good!

"What did you two do today?" Mrs. Giraux asked.

Jenny told her about exploring the neighborhood, visiting little shops, eating lunch in the open air. Then she rose and rummaged through the carrier of the stroller and pulled out several bags. It was fun to share her new purchases with someone. She missed her close friends in Whitney.

"I got a few more things to liven up this place. I can take them all with me when I head for home and they'll remind me of my summer here."

She unwrapped a lovely crystal vase which she placed on

the end table.

"I had to be so careful not to let this bump anything after I bought it but isn't it pretty? And look what else I found."

Two watercolors of Jackson Square were unveiled. Jenny leaned them against the chair. Then she withdrew a length of bright red and blue silk which she draped over one of the end tables.

"I love this. I don't have matching furniture at home so thought I could cover my end tables with this and no one would know."

"It's lovely. Set the vase on it. Ah, perfect. Now you need some flowers."

"I saw some at the flower stall I'd like, but I was too tired to stop," she said as she placed the vase just where she wanted it. "It will look great with a big bunch of cut flowers, won't it?"

"Indeed. Where's Jared?" Mrs. Giraux asked.

"Out on a date." Jenny was pleased her tone sounded so casual. Why shouldn't it? He could go on dates if he wanted. It was nothing to her!

Oh no? a small voice inside asked.

"On a date? Oh, my dear. I'm so sorry." Mrs. Giraux looked stricken.

"Mrs. G., I told you I'm here to care for Jamie. Nothing more. There's nothing between Jared and me."

The thought of that hot kiss filled her, but she pushed it away. And tried to ignore the feelings deep inside.

"I'm starving, but too tired to cook. Want to share a pizza?" Jenny asked, hoping to change the subject.

"Why, I'd like that. Thank you. It's been years since I've had a pizza." Mrs. Giraux smiled in anticipation.

"Shall we get one with everything on it?" Jenny asked.

"Of course. And I have some sweet tea at home. Let me dash across the hall to get it," the older woman said, reluctantly putting Jamie back in her carrier.

Chapter Fifteen

Jared sat on the wooden bench and gazed across the darkened water of the Mississippi. He stretched out his legs, wishing he could elevate his injured ankle. He'd done too much today. It ached. His ribs ached, too and he was bone weary.

But he didn't want to go home.

Jenny would be there.

She'd taken off that morning while he'd still been on the phone with Harry Simpson, one of the few men in the home office he knew well. He'd arranged to meet Harry and a couple of other guys after work. Then the day had stretched out endlessly. For the first time, Jared realized how much Jenny and the baby filled the hours.

She hadn't returned by the time he left and he wondered where she had gone and what she'd done all day. Had she made herself scarce because of their kiss?

Don't go there, he warned himself. He had hardly slept last night thinking about that kiss. And what he'd like to do with her if she came to him. He never asked women to his place— afraid of giving them ideas.

He scowled and gazed at the distant lights reflected on the slow-moving river.

Visiting with Harry and the others had been a bust. They

wanted to talk about wives and children. When one of them asked about Jared's family, they all seemed taken aback to discover Jared was still single. The jokes had flown after that, but he'd felt odd man out.

Heck, there were a lot of single men around. And he was sure glad he didn't have a desk job like Harry and the others.

But when Harry left after a couple of beers because he wanted to get home in time to have dinner with his family, Jared had felt a twinge of—what?

Envy?

Before long the other two men made arrangements to meet again, then said goodbye and departed. Both had wives to meet for dinner. The after-work drink was just a short stop before heading eagerly for home.

Jim had been like that when he moved in with Sohany. He and Jared had stopped doing things together after work. Sohany had been more important.

Jared hadn't let it bother him in the U.A.E., but now he considered what it meant to live his chosen lifestyle.

He was able to see the world or at least spots targeted for oil exploration. He'd vacationed in all the capitals in Europe, enjoyed the amenities on the French Riviera, seen the wonders of Venice and Florence.

Who cares for you? Jenny's words echoed in his mind and brought disquiet.

His family would care, if he didn't hold them away.

Jim had, once. But even that had taken a back seat during the last few months—once he had Sohany.

Jared suspected soft-hearted Jenny would care if he gave her the least bit of encouragement.

But it wasn't in the cards. He had what he wanted. And he

wasn't going to mess up a good thing by getting tied down again.

Never one for much introspection, he stood and headed for his apartment. It was the enforced inactivity that was driving him crazy. Things would be back to normal once he was fit.

The apartment was dark and quiet when he entered. A light shone over the stove in the kitchen. Its illumination the only bright spot in the place. Was Jenny already in bed? Or had she gone out?

He switched on the light near the door and listened. Nothing. He saw the stroller and bags. She was home. Had he expected her to greet him with open arms?

More fool him if he had.

He poured himself a tall glass of iced tea from the refrigerator and went to sit on the sofa. She'd been shopping again. The end table was covered in some filmy material, with a glass vase in the center. Next they'd have flowers, he suspected.

Some lacy concoction lay on the coffee table on top of one of his files.

There were two colorful paintings leaning against the chair that hadn't been there when he left. The material on the end table picked up the same hues. It wasn't much he acknowledged, but it did make the place seem more appealing. Friendlier.

Where did she plan to hang the pictures?

A noise caught his attention and he looked out on the balcony. She was sitting in the rocker. For a long minute he stared at her then rose and switched off the light. Crossing the living room, he stepped out to join her.

"I thought you were in bed already," he said, sinking

awkwardly to sit on the floor. Stretching out his legs, he almost gave a sigh of relief. It felt good. Leaning against the rough brick wall he studied the illuminated statue of Andrew Jackson through the wrought-iron railing.

Slowly the chair rocked back and forth.

"Not yet. I had dinner with Mrs. Giraux. We ordered in pizza. When she left, I came out here. It's the best time of day, warm but not hot. People still wandering around. I can hear music from the jazz clubs. You're back earlier than I expected."

"Harry wanted to get home to his family," he said evenly. "The others weren't far behind."

"Harry?" The rocking stopped and she looked at him.

He couldn't see her expression, but the faint light picked up the golden strands of hair. He tightened his grip on his glass. The longing to touch that silky hair was almost overwhelming.

Last night had not assuaged his hunger, only whetted it. He wanted to thread his fingers through the tresses again and feel the satiny texture.

Pull her onto his lap and kiss her until he forgot his name—as he almost had last night. Touch that warm skin, feel her catch of breath when she was excited. Know he could ignite her passion as she ignited his. He put the cold glass against his forehead, then looked at her.

"Harry Simpson, a man I know from the home office. A few of us got together for drinks after work. They brought me up to speed on what's happening at the site, the cleanup, the investigation. Reports are getting delayed, Harry and Phil had the latest skinny."

"Oh."

"I waited until almost five before I left. You still weren't home. Where did you go?"

"Just around. We explored every inch of the French Quarter. It was fun."

"We?"

"Jamie and me. She loves some of the shops."

"She told you so herself?"

Jenny laughed softly. "Well, she seemed fascinated by the colors and the sounds."

"And you seem fascinated as well. I see you bought some more things."

"Just a few. Things I can use in my apartment in Whitney when I go back. They'll remind me of my summer here." She paused, then asked, "So, what did the lawyer say?"

"I haven't called him yet."

"Why not? I thought you were going to call him today."

"I was thinking about what you said, that I'm her only tie to her parents. And while that's true, you know another explosion could finish me off unexpectedly like Jim. I'm going to write as much as I know about her parents."

"A family history for her to take with her?" she asked.

"You could say that. I'll see about getting some photographs while it won't cause any comments. Then I'll write what I remember about Sohany. I can still get in touch with her sister, I think, ask her some questions. Get as much information as I can for her to have. I hope the new parents tell her about her birth parents. They adored her."

"Sounds like a wonderful plan. Can I help?"

Her warmth confirmed her enthusiastic reception of his idea. Jared smiled in the darkness. How long would it take to write a biography?

"Are you any good at research?" It didn't matter. He'd take

whatever help she offered. He liked the idea of their working together.

"Only what I did in college, but won't most of the work involve writing down your memories of the two of them? How much research is in that?"

"I thought we might want to put something in about her grandparents as well—Jim's parents. There might be stuff in their obituaries that I don't know."

"You've thought this out."

It had just come to him, but he didn't need to tell her that. Improvising as he went along, he nodded.

"I don't expect it to take too long."

Jenny rocked a few minutes in silence, as if thinking about his proposal.

"You game?" he asked at last.

"Yes. I think it's a wonderful idea!"

"Good."

"Are you okay?" Jenny asked.

"Sure, why?"

"You sound, I don't know, tired I guess," she said.

"I am. My leg aches a bit"

"Couldn't be you overdid it today?" she teased. "Let me go get you some aspirin. How are your ribs feeling?"

"Don't fuss."

"Getting aspirin isn't fussing."

Jared watched her slip into the apartment. He could hear her run up the stairs. It had been a long time since anyone had taken care of him—even with something as minor as getting aspirin.

He kind of liked it.

In fact, he kind of liked having someone around. It wasn't

the same as when he was working. These days the hours hung heavy on his hands. It was pleasant to have her to share meals with, to talk to in the evening. He rarely sat out on the balcony before, now it was used frequently.

"Do you need water?" she called.

"No, I have iced tea."

"Here you go, then," she said coming back out.

He took the pills, brushing his fingers against her palm. He wanted to capture her hand, pull her down in his lap and see if she had made up her mind about another kiss.

But he swallowed the aspirin and said nothing. His body seemed to hum when she was near. He wished he could ignore the feelings that made him want her even more.

"Want to sit in the rocker?" she asked.

"No, it's better for my leg to be stretched out this way."

"I could get you a cushion. I bought a couple more for the sofa."

"I'm fine, Jenny. Sit back down."

There was a few minutes of silence, before Jenny broke it again.

"Mrs. Giraux crocheted a little lacy dress for Jamie. I left it on the coffee table so you can see it. It's so cute. And it won't be hot. She can wear it when your parents come if you like. Mrs. G. said she'd teach me how to crochet if I wanted."

"Mrs. Giraux is totally taken with Jamie."

"She adores her. She spent more time holding her this evening than eating. And the baby slept the entire time."

"Do you think she would mind watching her for us Friday night?"

"I don't think she'd mind. I expect she'd be thrilled. But why?"

"I've been invited to a barbeque party for the Fourth and I want you to come with me."

Jenny remained silent for so long Jared began to wonder if she'd heard him.

"Why me? Wouldn't you rather ask someone else?" she asked softly.

"No, I wouldn't rather ask someone else. If I'd wanted to, I would have done so. It's not that big a deal. A few of the men I know from the home office and their wives are getting together for the Fourth. Phil's hosting it at his place. It's just ribs and things."

"Okay, then. I'll ask Mrs. Giraux tomorrow and if she feels up to watching Jamie, I'll go."

"Good."

The aspirin seemed to be working. He didn't feel as achy as he had a little while ago. Of course, he still had to get up. But not yet. It wasn't that late.

"Are these old friends?" she asked a minute later.

"I've known Harry since I started with the firm. The others not as long. I don't know if I'll know everyone there on Friday. Most of the crowd there work for the company."

"Harry works here, in New Orleans?"

"Always has. He's a paper pusher."

"You make that sound awful."

Jared shrugged. "Not something I want to do."

"So what do you want to do? I mean for the next ten or twenty years. Or longer. Do you plan to live in foreign countries all your life? Exploring for oil?"

"Why not? I like it."

"So you've said. It's just hard for me to imagine. Isn't the desert rather barren after the lushness of Louisiana? I might like to visit a desert but I don't think I'd like to live there. What do you do? When you're not working, I mean?"

"This and that."

"That's specific. Really, I'd like to know."

He hesitated a minute, thinking about the last few months at the site. They were a hundred and seventy miles from Abu Dhabi, which was also the closest city of any size. Too far to make trips in during the week.

"I don't work only from nine to five," he said slowly. "There're always things to be done, paperwork to catch up on."

"That's it? Work?"

"Jim and I used to hang out together before Sohany came into his life. The company has a recreation center at the site."

"I'm not getting any picture here, Jared. Sounds like you wake up, go to work, come home and go to bed only to get up the next morning to go to work. What do you do for fun?"

"I like what I do for a living. It's hard to do much in an Arab country. There are a lot of restrictions. But every six or eight months I take a little R-and-R. Then I go some place in Europe."

"Oh."

Jared could tell Jenny wasn't impressed. And boiled down like that, it didn't sound impressive. What did he want to be doing in ten years? Still locating new sites for wells? Promotions could carry him only so far in the field. To really move up in the company, he'd need to eventually rotate into the home office.

"At least I'm not tied down like my father was," he said. "Or like my ex-wife wanted. I've seen Europe, a lot of the Middle East. I might take a vacation in Japan next year."

"Like you couldn't do all that working a regular job?

Doesn't your father take vacations?"

"Sure. He and Mom go somewhere every year."

"Then what does he have to feel tied down about? Sounds to me he probably gets more out of life than you. He at least has a family around to share the good times and the bad. I have to say, while I'd like to see some places in Europe, living in the great Arabian desert has never been something I think's cool. But don't listen to me. You know I want family and ties and roots and everything you don't want."

"And once you have that family, you'll be tied down."

"That's a state of mind. I can't see much difference between us, to be honest. If I want to travel to Europe, I could do so every summer. I have months off from teaching. But to go by myself sounds lonely. I'd rather stay home and do things with friends."

"Not me."

She laughed and rose. "We'll never agree on this. I'm going to check on Jamie. She should be waking for her last feeding soon. Good night."

Before he could answer, she was gone.

But her words echoed.

Chapter Sixteen

For the next two days Jenny and Jared worked on devising a family history for Jamie. He called the site office and requested some photos from Jim's file. A call to Sohany's sister gained a promise from her to send an assortment of photos of Jamie's mother. She asked if Jared in turn would send her one of her sister's only child.

"I think it must break her heart to have her niece so far away," Jenny said when he relayed the request.

He just looked at her, but Jenny knew he was probably scoffing at how she viewed things. She didn't care. She liked herself just as she was, romantic views and all.

They discovered they would be able to use interlibrary borrowing to obtain microfilms of the Whitney newspaper. She was impressed with the lengths Jared was willing to go to compile this information for Jamie.

In addition to obtaining facts and photos, he spent a lot of time telling Jenny about growing up with Jim, the escapades they shared as boys, the traveling they'd done together as men. She jotted notes—wishing there had been someone who had known her parents. Someone who had done as much for her.

Jenny began to wonder if Jared was ever going to call his attorney. Not that she planned to remind him. It had been more than a week now since he'd returned home. She'd seen no effort on his part to even alert his attorney as to his plans, much less implement the necessary paperwork.

She was beginning to suspect Jared was not as anxious to be relieved of his responsibility as he claimed to be.

Maybe as he grew to know Jamie, he was falling under her spell. She was a darling baby, and Jenny knew anyone who met her would love her.

"It isn't as if he doesn't like you," she explained to Jamie when she bathed her Friday morning. Jamie's splashes and kicking feet soaked them both, but Jenny loved this time with the two of them.

"It's just he doesn't know much about being around babies. I think you make him nervous."

Jenny almost laughed at the thought of Jared being afraid of an infant. He was strong, capable, focused, able to deal with the myriad of problems at an oil site—used to directing men, comfortable with his mantle of authority.

Maybe for that reason he was uneasy about a tiny baby— he had so little experience dealing with children. And Jamie was totally unimpressed with his authority. As long as he fed her when she was hungry, she was content.

"Jared!" she called, rinsing Jamie, laughing when the baby's fist splashed in the shallow water showering the spray over her shirt.

"What?" He appeared in the doorway.

"I didn't get her clothes. Can you hold her while I go find something for her to wear?"

He looked at the baby, then frowned. Shaking his head, he stepped back. "I'll find her something to wear. Where are her things?"

"I know right where everything is. I want her to wear that little red and white outfit today. Come on and hold her in the tub and let her play in the water a bit longer. She's all clean so you don't have to wash her."

Gingerly he slid his hand where Jenny's had been, supporting the baby's back and head. "Hurry up."

Jenny eased her hands out, conscious of Jared's closeness. His attention was focused on Jamie, but Jenny felt a tug of attraction. Her knees almost buckled.

For a split second she let herself imagine they were a family. Dangerous thoughts, but the image wouldn't fade. He'd help out with their baby. Together they'd enjoy watching Jamie grow. She'd love making a home for the three of them.

Maybe they'd have an additional baby or two.

Stunned at the intensity of her feelings, she quickly dried her hands and hurried into her bedroom seeking a moment of privacy. It was one thing to yearn for a family of her own, something else again to see one where it was impossible. She'd only set herself up for disappointment and heartache if she continued dreaming along those lines.

Jared Montgomery was not the man for her. Even if he'd come to care for her, kept Jamie and proposed making the three of them into a family, would she ever know if it was true love or expediency? If he decided he could raise Jamie, he'd need to look around for a wife. And who better than someone Jamie already knew?

If she could work a miracle, he'd never make that call to the attorney.

But that didn't mean he'd fall in love with her, either!

And she'd vowed only to marry for love.

When Jenny returned a couple of minutes later she swore

Jared had not moved an inch. Smiling despite herself, she nudged him.

"Okay, I've got her clothes. Lift her out and I'll dry her off." She drew the towel from the rack.

"Lift her? She's as slippery as an eel," he said. "I'll drop her."

"No, you won't. Just make sure you're holding her securely."

She opened the towel and reached for the baby.

Jared scooped her up and almost threw her into Jenny's waiting arms. Snugly wrapping the baby in the towel, Jenny looked at him. "Want to watch while I get her dressed?"

He shook his head. "Next time remember to bring the clothes." He dumped the water from the baby's bath into the tub. Before she could argue the point, the phone rang.

"Saved by the bell," he said, moving as swiftly as his cast allowed down the steps.

Reluctantly she conceded defeat. Another day, maybe.

Settling Jamie down, Jenny quickly tidied up the bathroom and then wandered downstairs. Jared was still on the phone. Not wishing to eavesdrop, she walked out on the balcony.

Leaning on the railing, feeling the warmth of the black wrought iron, she considered what she might do in the afternoon. She'd already explored most of the shops within walking distance. Seen some of the not-to-be-missed sights of the French Quarter.

"That was my mother, reminding me that she and my father will be arriving by lunchtime tomorrow," Jared said as he joined her on the balcony.

"Did she think you'd forget?" Jenny asked.

Resting his own hands on the railing, the edge of his right

hand touched the edge of her left. Jenny felt the contact to her toes. She wanted to snatch her hand away, put at least ten feet between them. Or move even closer and see what another kiss would bring.

She almost covered his hand with hers. The desire to lace her fingers through his, tug until he stood so close every inch of his body was pressed against hers was almost more than she could withstand. That's what she missed not being part of a couple. The give and take of every day life would be more fun with someone to love.

She hadn't forgotten one second of that kiss. And every cell within her yearned for another. Too bad she couldn't get her mind and body to coordinate. She knew intellectually Jared would never be for her. Yet her traitorous body seemed to ignore that fact and clamor for what it should definitely not have.

"I'm sure she's worried about you," she said a minute later, pleased her voice sounded normal. Time seemed to have no meaning. She could only focus on the spiraling sensations that started where her hand touched his, raced up her arm and swirled around inside. She couldn't think of anything to say that wouldn't give her tumbling emotions away.

"So she said. I should have warned her about the baby. She's excited to see her. She asked me all sorts of questions about her."

"That's normal with a grandmother. And you said you hadn't told them the full story. Do you plan to tell them when you see them?"

"I don't know yet. It's complicated. She also has a passel of questions about you," he said with a sideway glance at her.

"Me?" Jenny looked at him, glad for the excuse to remove

her hand. Much longer in such close contact and she'd become a blithering idiot. "What did she ask about me?"

"How you were doing caring for an infant." He crossed his arms across his chest and glared at the statue across the square. "If she's matchmaking again, I'll send them both packing as soon as they arrive. Patti was supposed to make sure they knew I only needed someone to watch the baby until other arrangements could be made."

Jenny forced a laugh. "Surely your mother must know by now that you have no intentions of getting married. But I think you should explain the situation with Jamie to them as soon as they arrive. They'll be incredibly hurt if they think Jamie's your daughter and you're giving her up for adoption."

"If I know my mother, she'll try to talk me out of it regardless of whose baby it is. She'll probably offer to take Jamie herself."

"That might be a solution," Jamie said slowly.

If the Montgomerys raised Jamie in Whitney, Jenny would get to see the baby as she grew up. Maybe even teach her first grade class.

The phone rang again.

"Guess people know you're back," she said.

"Don't run off, I want to talk to you about this visit," he said as he headed in for the phone.

Jenny sat in the rocker in a sliver of shade almost convinced that Jared didn't have a clue how she felt about him. He made no mention of their blazing hot kiss. Nor pressed for another.

Of course he had said the next step was up to her, but what did he expect—she'd come right out and ask for another kiss? A woman liked to have some clue to how a man felt.

Dare she let herself be sidetracked from her goal of finding the right man? Even for a brief summer romance?

A few minutes later Jenny realized it was silent in the living room—no murmur of Jared's voice. Had he finished the phone call? She peeked in. Jared sat on the sofa, the phone had been hung up.

Something about his expression made her curious. She walked into the cool room and sat on the edge of the easy chair facing him. He didn't even look up.

"Who was it?" she asked.

"Margaret, Jim's widow."

"Oh, dear."

"She heard from my mother that I was back. She wants to come see me—to talk about Jim," Jared said, rubbing his eyes with his thumb and forefinger.

"Uh-oh," Jenny said softly.

"Yeah. What a mess! What am I going to tell her?"

"Do you think she's going to ask about Jamie?" Jenny wanted to snatch the baby up and protect her.

"She has no reason to know anything about the baby. She said she wanted to hear how Jim had spent the last months, weeks, days."

"Tough on you," Jenny said sympathetically. "When's she coming?"

"She didn't say—just soon. After my parents visit. It's just one thing after another."

"You'll survive," she said dryly.

He looked at her with a gleam in his eye. "I'd survive a lot easier if I had someone on my side."

"Like?"

Her smile came slow. She suspected what he was up to—

or at least hoped. Maybe this was the sign she was looking for.

"Such as a housemate who would be more than willing to stand with me."

"Oh, I can stand with you." She hesitated a moment, then took the plunge. "It's the other part I'm waiting for."

"Other part?" Jared asked, leaning over to take her hand in his, lacing his fingers with hers.

"The part that comes in addition to the standing by," she said, feeling that familiar turmoil. Forgetting everything but the man who sat in front of her, she decided to let the future take care of itself. Right now she was more interested in the present.

"And that is?"

"You tell me?"

"Well, we could become comrades in arms," he suggested, tugging her off the chair and onto the sofa.

"What did you have in mind?" She was breathless.

But instead of answering her, he pulled her into his arms. His mouth descended on hers before she could say a word.

The kiss was brief, all too brief, Jenny thought a few seconds later. She lay against his chest, gazing up into his eyes. The teasing had enticed. The kiss made her yearn for more.

"I thought you were going to wait for me to make the next move," she said, her fingers tracing the muscles beneath his shirt.

"You took too long," he said, his mouth covering hers again.

This time the kiss seemed endless. No longer content with a brief brush of lips, Jared deepened the kiss. He tightened his hold on her until she felt every inch of his chest against her. Slowly they toppled over until they were lying on the sofa.

Jenny opened her mouth to kiss him back. It was glorious.

She wished it could go on forever. Ignoring the whispers of doubt, she gave herself up to the pure pleasure of his embrace.

When his hands moved across her back, she arched closer. The intensity of her responses startled her. Why was this one man able to drive her to the edge? Raise her to heights never known before? And fill her with such a longing to draw even closer?

Jenny began to wonder where it would all lead when Jared ended the kiss and looked at her. His thumb rubbed against her lower lip, the touch sending jolts of awareness through her already fevered body. She touched the tip with her tongue and was rewarded with a quiet groan from him.

"You're potent stuff," Jared said softly. "Enough to make a man forget a lot in a short time."

Jenny pushed back and sat up, smoothing down her shirt.

Was that all he wanted—a few minutes to forget the problems that were piling up? Forget that Margaret wanted some of his time and memories? Forget his parents' impending visit and their expected pressures regarding Jamie?

"Glad I could help," she said, starting to rise.

He yanked her back on the sofa.

"Wait a minute. What's going on? One minute you're an active participant, now you're getting huffy?"

Jenny leveled him a look. "Thanks for giving me a few minutes escape from the duties of the summer."

"What?" He looked thunderstruck. "Is that all it was for you?"

"I thought that's all it was for you. That's what your comment made me feel," she said. "It was a mind- blowing kiss as you very well know. Then you said it made you forget for a time. Gee, thanks."

He smiled that lopsided smile that had her toes curling, her heart racing.

"Forgot my name, I think."

"And everything else going on."

"That wasn't the reason I kissed you."

"Then what was?"

"I wanted to. I want you."

She stared at him for endless seconds. Her mind echoed his words as she tried to take it all in. Tried to decide what she wanted, what she needed.

"It's not possible," she said slowly, longing to have him argue the point. For him to come up with a compelling reason why it could be.

"It's a great idea. You just need to get used to it," he said.

"I can't believe you! It would complicate things to death. We are not getting involved."

So saying, she jumped up and crossed the room, as if putting distance between them could erase the feelings that still clamored for release. As if the width of a room could end the yearning to have his mouth on hers again, end the desire to feel his mouth caressing her again.

"So we go back to waiting until you're ready. Just don't take too long," he said leaning negligently back against the sofa cushions.

She wanted to stamp her foot and yell and scream— then dash back across the room and wipe that arrogant grin from his face.

Instead, Jenny went quickly upstairs to check on the baby, annoyed at his cocky comment. If he thought she was just playing games, he had another think coming! She was not going to fall for him.

She was not!

Seeing the baby was still sleeping, she reluctantly went back down stairs. She was not going to sulk in her room or feel restricted from moving around the apartment if she wanted.

Jared was working at the computer again.

"Come read this and see if it makes sense to you. I got some info from Sohany's sister and another picture. This one of their entire family. Maybe Jamie will never get to know her maternal grandparents, but she'll know what they look like."

So they were going to ignore things for the good of the project. That worked for her.

Chapter Seventeen

Jenny thought about Jared's provocative comment at least a hundred times by the time she dropped the baby at Mrs. Giraux's that evening. She'd tried to keep busy all day, adding to the biography, washing out the baby's things, pressing some clothes of her own that really didn't need it. Anything to push the tantalizing thoughts from her mind.

To no avail. It remained front and center.

She went over everything pertaining to Jamie's care with her neighbor, delighting in Mrs. Giraux's enthusiasm at watching the child. Giving Mrs. Giraux her cell number, she told her to call if she had any questions or concerns. Jenny made sure she knew where they'd be and gone over all instructions at least twice.

She still had trouble walking away. How did mothers do it?

"She'll be fine with me," Mrs. Giraux said gently. "And I really look forward to doing this. I used to watch Samuel's nephews when they were little. If anything comes up, I'll call you right away."

Not wanting the woman to think she didn't trust her, Jenny smiled and left.

"I think I'm feeling separation anxiety," Jenny said a few

minutes later as she and Jared walked slowly toward Royal Street and her car.

He carried the cane, but she noted he rarely used it. He still limped with the walking cast, but most of the bruises around his face had faded.

Glancing at the apartment once more over her shoulder, she caught Jared's amused gaze.

"What?" She flushed, feeling silly.

She knew Mrs. Giraux was perfectly capable of caring for Jamie for a few hours.

"That's what I'd ask. What's the problem? Mrs. Giraux has been dying to watch Jamie. The kid'll sleep most of the time. She knows the woman, so won't be upset when she wakes. You gave her your phone number so she can reach us if there's an emergency. What's the problem?"

"Maybe it's a woman thing," Jenny murmured, knowing in her mind everything was fine. It was her heart that already missed the baby.

Jared reached out and caught her arm, halting her. "If you don't want to leave her, I'm sure Phil won't mind if we bring her along."

Jenny shook her head and tried to smile.

"I'm being totally silly. Jamie's much better staying with Mrs. Giraux than at a gathering of strangers where she could get off schedule. Or catch something. Let's go."

If she missed the baby this much when leaving for an evening, what was she going to do when her summer job ended? When Jared found a loving home for Jamie and no longer needed her to watch the baby?

She loved that little girl, felt a special bond. While she fervently wished the best for Jamie, she also wished she could be a part of her life—at least to the extent of knowing she was well loved and cared for.

Comrades in arms, Jared had said before he kissed her that afternoon. But he meant only for a few weeks. It wasn't as if they'd keep in touch once he returned to the Middle East.

Tonight wasn't a date. He was going to visit coworkers he knew from his company. She was more like a glorified chauffeur.

And she'd do well to keep that in mind!

The Friday night traffic in the French Quarter was already heavy. Jenny maneuvered skillfully through the vehicles clogging the streets, knowing she'd be lucky to find a parking place anywhere near the apartment when they returned.

"Do any of the men who'll be at the barbeque tonight work in the field with you?" she asked.

"A couple did when they first started, but all of them now work in the home office," Jared said, glancing at her. "Why?"

"Just wondered. Are any special friends?"

"I see a couple of them each time I'm in town. Harry and I have known each other the longest."

"And they're all married?"

"Every last one of them."

Jenny drove in silence for a while.

"Now what are you thinking?" he asked suspiciously after several moments of silence.

"Just trying to figure out why I'm included in this. I suspect so you don't have to be odd man out, right? Or was it to get a ride?"

"Can't I want you to come to spend the evening with me?"

She flicked him a wry glance. "Jared, we've been spending several evenings together. I didn't have to come to this. I'd think you'd be tired of me by now."

He was silent for a few moments, then stared out the windshield. "I wanted you there."

"Okay."

Jenny felt frustrated. She got such mixed messages from the man!

Sometimes she believed he truly liked her and wanted to spend time with her.

Then something would happen and he'd grow distant and aloof.

It drove her nuts.

When they turned onto Phil's street, Jenny noticed the newness of all the homes and the similar design. Tracts were good and well and for people who loved new homes they were perfect. She'd prefer an older home in a neighborhood that had had time for trees to mature and shrubs to grow.

Phil and his wife Joline met them at the door.

"Glad you made it, Jared. And this pretty lady is?" Phil smiled as he held out his hand.

"My friend Jenny," Jared said, his own arm coming around Jenny's shoulders in a proprietorial manner. The sundress she wore left her shoulders bare and his palm was warm against her skin.

Hiding her surprise at the description, Jenny greeted Phil and his wife. Before long she and Jared were in the backyard with the other guests, moving from group to group, meeting everyone, chatting for a little while before moving on.

"So are you thinking of giving up the dangers of site work and settling back in the home office now?" Harry asked Jared when everyone was seated at the two huge picnic tables set up for dining. Jared sat on one end to accommodate his cast and

Jenny sat between him and Harry.

"I have no plans to. They're expecting me back once the ankle heals."

"How do you like his being gone all the time?" Harry asked Jenny. "Has to play havoc with courting."

Jenny blinked, then opened her mouth to reply. Before she said a word, however, Jared spoke.

"Jenny understands that a man has to go where his work is. It's not a problem with us, is it?"

She shook her head, hiding a smile. "Not at all."

What was he up to?

When Harry spoke to the woman on his far side, she leaned close to Jared, keeping her voice low.

"Courting?" she said and almost giggled. "First I've heard of it."

"If it makes them happy thinking that, why not?"

"Well, I could think of a bunch of reasons, actually."

"It can't hurt to let them presume that for one night."

"But no reason to presume that which I can see."

He started to say something but the woman across from her spoke and Jenny turned to her to respond. Before long they were talking about children—hers and the ones Jenny had in her classes. Jenny's experience as a teacher gave her plenty of anecdotes to share that had the others laughing.

"Hey, Jared, what's this rumor we've heard at the office that you came home with a baby?" one of the men at the other table called.

Jenny looked at him, waiting for Jared to field that one.

"That's right," he said evenly, his gaze challenging anyone to say another word.

Jenny wondered if she could get him to teach her that

expression—it would probably work wonders with the rambunctious boys in her class. It worked here, the topic was immediately dropped.

Dropped but not forgotten, she thought a few minutes later when she volunteered to get Jared and herself some iced tea. She stood in line behind two women to wait her turn at the large frosty pitcher of sweet tea at the end of the buffet table. They spoke softly, but not so quietly she couldn't hear them.

"...said he heard the baby was Jared's and the mother died."

"Makes you wonder, doesn't it? First time since we've known him he's brought a woman to one of these things. Must want a mother for that baby pretty badly."

"Sure, marry her, dump the kid on her and then take off for the Middle East again. He should have thought things through before having a baby."

From the strongly disapproving tone, Jenny knew Jared hadn't won points by keeping quiet about Jim and Sohany. How much would his reputation suffer when he gave the baby up for adoption?

She longed to set the women straight, but knew it wasn't her place to reveal Jared's secret. Doing so with Mrs. G had been one thing. At the time she hadn't known it was a secret. Revealing it here might cause it to get back to Jim's wife.

But it hurt her to hear them discuss him so callously. If they knew what a good man he was, that he had the baby's best interest at heart, wouldn't they change their opinions?

Jenny stepped up to the iced tea pitcher as they moved away and the thought struck that she should keep an open mind about Jared herself. He was doing what he sincerely thought was in Jamie's best interest He didn't plan to stay in the States, and rather than consign Jamie to a relationship with a once-a-year daddy, he was trying to provide her with loving, constant parents.

To stay and be a true parent to the baby would mean changing his entire life. And Jenny couldn't see asking that of any man. For the first time she truly began to see Jared's plan as possibly a good solution for his friend's baby.

Jared glanced over toward the buffet table to check on Jenny. There were several people mingling near the end. She stood waiting patiently to get their tea. He felt impatience rise and turned back to Phil and Harry as they compared their sons' prowess in Little League.

Some of the stories the men told had Jared remembering his own baseball games during the long summers when he was growing up. His father had pitched endless practice balls so Jared could perfect his batting. One year they'd worked on his fielding. Now he listened as Harry bragged about playing with his son.

Listening only half-heartedly, Jared wondered if little girls grew up liking baseball. Would Jamie be thrilled with the game or prefer to play with dolls and tea party sets?

Her dad had loved sports. Many times Jared and Jim had played pickup games at the various sites they'd worked on.

Another reason to miss Jim.

He'd have to remember to add that to the biography he was writing.

"Here you go, icy cold." Jenny set the tall glass on the table in front of him. Smiling at the men who had gravitated to that end she inclined her head toward the other table.

"I'm going over there to talk with Joline and the others,"

she said.

He nodded and watched her walk across the grass.

"You've got it bad," Harry said, slapping Jared on the shoulder.

"Real bad," Mark agreed, his grin wide.

Jared looked back. "Meaning?"

"Meaning you can't keep your eyes off her. When's the big date?"

Jared shrugged and sipped the iced tea. He took their teasing in the spirit it was meant and tried to ignore it. No sense in stirring up things by telling them he was not the marrying kind. If they didn't know that by now, nothing he said would convince them otherwise.

Especially not after letting everyone think there was something between him and Jenny.

"Time you came in from the field. We could use your knowledge in the home office," Phil said.

"Don't want to wait too long between kids, either," one of the other men said. "That little girl of yours will be growing fast and you'll want the other children close enough in age to have something in common as they grow up."

"Or bicker all the time, like mine do," another called.

"Are you rotating back?" Harry asked.

"Don't have any plans to," Jared said. "I like the excitement of field work."

"Man, it's got to get old," Phil said. "I did a stretch a few years back. Couldn't wait to get home. I don't speak the language, missed American cooking, television. Going out for a beer with friends. You've got to miss that, Jared."

"Sometimes," he acknowledged. "But I'm used to it."

"I'll bet you'll get used to living here again really fast. By the time your ankle's healed, you'll be wishing you could stay."

Jared shrugged. He doubted it. The last time he'd been in New Orleans, he'd counted the days until he could get back to work.

"Jenny'll make the difference from now on," Harry said confidently.

"Do you think so?" Jared asked, trying to ignore the sensations sweeping through him at the thought of a long-term affair with Jenny. He hadn't fallen in love since Andrea. He let the thought sink in.

He frowned.

He wasn't falling in love with her. He was attracted to her, that's all.

"When you're footloose and fancy-free, one place is as good as another. But once you've found someone special, you want to be with that person. And we all know women don't go to the Middle East. If you still like the rigs, we've got a dozen in the Gulf which are a lot closer to home than the U.A.E." Philip said.

"I'm too young to be tied down," Jared said, half joking. He didn't like the serious turn to the conversation.

Phil slapped him on the back again and rose. "Don't wait too long, my friend or all the good women will be gone. Can I get anyone anything?"

"Not for me. We've got to get going. The kids have a full day tomorrow," Harry said, also rising.

Jared watched with a sense of relief as the couples in the yard begin to gather their things in preparation for leaving. He was ready to go as well.

"I liked your friends," Jenny said a few minutes later as they headed for home. The streets were less crowded than earlier, but she knew the Quarter would be jammed. "Especially Joline and Cathy. Both of them recommended I try for a job teaching here in New Orleans."

"Haven't you already signed a contract for next year in Whitney?" he asked. Why would she consider moving to New Orleans? Her home was in Whitney. Her friends. There was nothing here for her. Except distance from that guy who let her down.

"Not yet. We get them the first of August. I know I'm going to be offered one, despite the economy."

"You're better staying where you know people."

"Like you?" she mocked.

He shook his head. "I didn't want to live in Whitney. Andrea and I had an apartment near Metairie. We did all the things newlyweds are supposed to do. Only she loved it and I hated it."

"Why marry to begin with, then?"

"It seemed the thing to do at the time."

"Didn't you love her?"

He looked at her in the darkness of the car, her face illuminated from time to time as lights from passing vehicles shone in.

"I thought I did. Just as I thought she loved me. But when push came to shove, we didn't want the same things. I wanted to travel, see some of the world, use my knowledge of geology. She wanted a man who was home every minute he wasn't at work. It was— claustrophobic."

"Then you were right to separate, to end the marriage before you both became bitter and unhappy. I'm in Andrea's camp on this, however. I'd expect my husband home when not at work, too. But only because he wanted to be there with me. Not out of a sense of duty," she said thoughtfully.

"Let me give you a hint. If you find this perfect paragon, cut him some slack. He'll be a person in his own right. Give him some space," Jared said.

"Noted," she said dryly.

"Noted but not believed?"

"Yes, I believe I shouldn't cling. But I expect my husband will wish to spend time with me. Otherwise, why marry? Two people could date for all that. What happened to Andrea?"

"She married a welder and they live in Baton Rouge. They have two or three kids, last I heard."

"So she got what she wanted. Is she happy?"

"So my mother says. She hears from her from time to time. Her parents still live in Whitney and she stops by to see my folks sometimes."

He'd had no communications with her since the divorce. He'd been glad when his mother told him once about her marriage. It sounded as if she'd gotten just what she wanted the second time around.

Chapter Eighteen

Jenny wanted to ask if Jared was also happy, suspecting he'd snap a quick affirmation. But deep down, didn't he get lonely? Didn't he wish to have one special someone to be there for him?

Or didn't men care about that as strongly as women did? Was he truly content to roam the globe all his life?

"I knew the traffic would be terrible when we got back," she murmured as she turned on Royal Street and had to wait several minutes before inching forward. Revelers wandered across the street at will. Cars double-parked. Others tied up traffic unloading passengers. People with drinks in hand staggered along the sidewalk. The sounds of music blared from nightclubs, sounding disconnected as each song vied for dominance in the night.

Inching along, she searched in vain for an open parking place.

"I may have to drop you at the apartment and try farther afield," she said as she turned onto another crowded street.

"Forget it. You're not walking alone around here at night. I can walk as far as you can. The cast is designed for it."

"But you've been on your feet a lot today, aren't you tired?"

"Not too tired to make sure you have an escort. Don't you

have a clue how dangerous this area can be after dark? I want to make sure you get home safely."

Even wearing a cast, he was more than capable of defending her against anything that threatened. Jenny nodded, a feeling of warmth washing through her. Normally there was no one in her life to even know if she was out late, much less show concern.

They were ten blocks away from the apartment when she found a space and zipped into it just as the previous occupant was pulling out.

"This is fun," she said as they walked along the crowded sidewalks back to the apartment, smiling at the other people out to enjoy the evening.

"Too many tourists," he grumbled, putting an arm around her shoulders and pulling her close, out of the way of a boisterous group lunging down the sidewalk. He didn't like the way some of the men looked at her.

"All the tourists make it exciting. Ever been here during Mardi Gras?"

"A couple of times—when I was younger. It's wild then."

"I'd like to be here once. Tad brought us down for a weekend last Spring, but not at Mardi Gras."

He didn't like the reminder she had another life, of which he had no part. Nor the fact she'd been close to another man.

What else had she and Tad done when visiting? Had they seen all the sights? Had he taken her on a carriage ride around the Vieux Carre and kissed her?

The thought burned. The few kisses they'd shared had only whetted his appetite for more.

But not tonight.

The timing was bad. His parents were due to arrive in the

morning. He'd be obligated to spend some time with them.

But once the weekend was over, it would be just the two of them again. And if she didn't object, he'd move ahead—not waiting for her to make up her mind. Time was growing short. He wanted her before he left. With enough kisses, wouldn't she admit she desired him as much as he did her?

He wanted to discover what being together could mean. To discover all he could about her. And not in a physical sense. He liked being surprised by her thoughts and ideas--innocent and romantic as they often were. He enjoyed the unexpected comments she made. There was more to Jenny Stratford than met the eye.

Mrs. Giraux opened the door to her apartment immediately when Jenny knocked. Jared unlocked his door as Jenny went in to get Jamie.

"She was a perfect angel," Mrs. Giraux said softly. "We had a lovely evening together. And I just fed her a little while ago, so she should sleep through until morning."

"Thank you, Mrs. G. We really appreciate this. I missed her," Jenny confessed as they tiptoed to where Jamie lay sleeping in the stroller. Slowly Jenny began pushing it to the door.

"Call me anytime. I really enjoyed it. Did you have a nice evening?" Mrs. Giraux asked as she went to the door with Jenny.

"I had a great time. It was interesting to meet people Jared knows. I don't know if he had as good a time. Once or twice I caught him frowning--whether from his ankle aching or due to the conversation, I don't know."

"Come over tomorrow and tell me all about it," the older woman invited.

"If I can. Jared's parents will be here tomorrow. They haven't seen her yet."

Jenny hesitated then looked at the older woman with troubled eyes. "I think he's going to tell them Jamie isn't his and that he's giving her up for adoption."

"Nonsense, child. He wouldn't do something like that. He's still feeling his way. Much as he talks about it, if he were going to do anything, it would have been done before now."

"I wish I had your faith in that. Anyway, I'm going to the Café du Monde to pick up beignets for our breakfast, would you like to join us?"

"Thank you, Jenny. I would like that." She smiled in anticipation.

A moment later Jenny pushed the stroller into Jared's apartment.

"I see she survived your being away," he said opening the door to the balcony. The apartment was warm and the opened door allowed a breeze to filter in.

"Yes. Mrs. Giraux loved watching her."

"So if we need a sitter another night, she'd be willing?" he asked, his gaze on the baby.

"Why would we?" Jenny looked at him in surprise.

"I don't know. Just asking. If my folks insist we go out to dinner or something. It'd be good to know in advance."

"I'm sure she would. I invited her for breakfast tomorrow. What time are your parents arriving?"

"Sometime before lunch."

"Plenty of time, then, in the morning to get Jamie ready. I'll take her up now. Thanks, for taking me tonight. I enjoyed it."

"The night's young, Jenny. Come back down," he said softly.

She hesitated on the bottom step then shook her head. "Not tonight, Jared. It's late and I'm tired. I'll see you in the morning."

Coward, she chided herself as she climbed the steps, holding on tightly to Jamie. She longed to dash back downstairs and see what Jared had in mind. It involved kissing, she just knew it. And more, if he had his way. But as much as she wanted to, she couldn't do it

Gently laying the baby in the crib, she pulled up the light blanket and patted her back for a couple of moments. Oh, to be young and innocent and have all her needs met without even asking.

Slowly Jenny prepared for bed, discarding her dress, pulling on an old comfortable sleep shirt. She didn't know what she wanted. Her mind knew she should remember Jared would be leaving soon. That he was not marrying material. And even if he was, he wasn't for her.

But she longed to feel his kisses. Longed to explore the feelings and emotions that bubbled to the surface anytime she was around him.

Anytime she thought of him.

Just because they both wanted different things in life didn't mean they couldn't have a summer of memories which could last her forever.

Would he think of her in the future? Or would she be one in a long line of women with whom he shared only a part of himself?

Would part be enough? she wondered as she drifted to sleep.

Sometime later Jenny awoke to Jamie's cries.

She threw back the sheet and hurried to the baby's crib.

Picking up the little girl, she patted her back.

"What's the matter, sweetie?"

Since the first night, the baby had slept through until around five. Glancing at the clock Jenny noted it was only twenty minutes to four. Too early for Jamie to awaken. Only no one had told Jamie.

Working up to screams, the baby fussed around and cried.

Crooning to her, Jenny started to change her diapers. They were wet—enough to awaken her?

"What's going on?" Jared asked from the doorway to her room. "She's screaming loud enough to wake the dead!"

"I don't know. I'm changing her. If that doesn't work, I guess I'll try a bottle. She usually sleeps longer."

He watched them for a couple of minutes. The baby cried, waving her fists, kicking her legs. Despite Jenny's soothing, she would not calm down. Jenny appeared to be having difficulty fastening the diapers.

"I'll start a bottle. At least the nipple in her mouth will keep her quiet," he said.

"Thanks. I'll bring her down in a minute," Jenny said, trying to capture one leg to put in the sleeper.

When Jenny and Jamie arrived in the kitchen a few minutes later, Jared was still warming the bottle. Jenny looked at him, awareness slamming in her. He wore only a pair of shorts. His cast covered the lower part of one leg. Otherwise all she could see was glorious golden skin.

His chest and shoulders were muscular, providing concrete proof he was not a paper-jockey but actually worked in the field. His tan hadn't faded, but was deep and rich. She had felt those muscles beneath his shirt, now her fingertips itched to trace that smooth expanse of skin, feel the solid strength beneath.

Bouncing the baby a bit, she realized she wore only an old T-shirt. Soft and worn, it hugged her skin— ending mid-thigh.

When Jared looked at her, she wished she'd put on a robe, or changed into shorts or a dress. His gaze trailed across her, down her long legs, back up again. The wicked glint in his eyes should have warned her, but instead it excited her.

She rocked Jamie, trying to calm her, but the baby continued to cry. Her own heart raced, heat swept through like a bolt of lightening. Her gaze locked with Jared's and the rest of the kitchen faded. Even Jamie's cries seemed to diminish. Jenny was conscious of only Jared and the hot desire in his gaze.

Jenny knew she had to remember–he was a solitary man, going his own way alone and unencumbered. She wanted a home and family in the worst way.

But something was right for them at this moment and she'd be a fool to let it slip away.

"Here, it's ready." He tested the milk, then handed her the bottle. Jenny cradled Jamie in her arms and in seconds the infant was feeding like she was starved.

"Mrs. Giraux fed her at eleven, she said. I don't know why Jamie woke up so hungry," Jenny said, watching the baby eat rather than let her gaze clash with Jared's again. She had to focus on the child in her arms at least until she went back to the crib.

"It doesn't matter. It looks as if the milk's what she wanted. Once she eats, she'll go back to sleep."

Jared stood near enough to Jenny and the baby to smell the scent of talc, the sweet floral fragrance of Jenny's perfume. Did she wear it all over her body, or just dab it around her ears and throat? He longed to find out.

That silky blond hair gleamed in the overhead light. He brushed it back, letting the strands trail across his fingers. She looked up and Jared stared into her bright blue eyes. Jenny Stratford was beautiful.

Leaning forward a little, he brushed his lips across hers. He longed to pull her into his arms, but the baby still drank from her bottle. He could wait until she finished.

Impatiently he silently urged the baby to finish.

"She eats slow," he growled.

Jenny laughed softly, the sound reaching deep inside him. He liked her smile, her laugh, her sunny disposition. She was captivating.

"She'll be finished soon enough."

"Not soon enough," he argued.

Kissing her again, he felt her mouth move against his, open for a deeper kiss.

How was he going to keep from crushing her in his arms while she held Jamie? He wanted to feel that soft body pressed against his. Wanted to have Jenny's arms encircle his neck, to feel her squeeze against him until there wasn't a breath of anything between them.

"Here, hold this." Jenny handed him the bottle and placed Jamie on her shoulder, rubbing her back gently.

"We could go upstairs," she suggested. "Then as soon as she's done, I can pop her into the crib."

"I like the way you think," he said, brushing a kiss on her free shoulder, tugging the old cotton shirt to one side as his lips caressed her creamy skin.

"Good. Because I'm having trouble with that," she said, turning her head and brushing her lips across his cheek.

"What?"

"Thinking when you're touching me like that."

Jared smiled and trailed kisses up her neck.

When the baby burped, he pulled back and smiled down into Jenny's eyes. "There's a statement."

"For or against?"

"Once she's fed, I doubt she'll care one way or the other. Do you?"

Jared laughed and hugged her, baby and all.

They looked at Jamie. Her black eyes gazed solemnly up at them.

"I don't think she's sucking as strongly as she was. Maybe she's getting full," Jenny said doubtfully, her heart racing as she stood in Jared's embrace.

"I think she's deliberately taking her time."

"She's a baby, what does she know?"

"Look at her. Her eyes have a definite gleam in them. She's toying with us."

Jenny laughed softly. "You're seeing things."

Finally Jamie was sated. Burped, double-checked for dry diapers. Jenny laid her in the crib. To her immense relief, the baby snuggled right down and closed her eyes.

The light was switched off.

Turning, Jenny tried to see Jared in the faint light coming in through the window.

"I'm sorry she woke you," Jenny said, seeing his outline in the doorway.

"I'm good with it if I get a kiss goodnight," he relied.

She doubted the wisdom of a kiss in the dark with both wide awake, but couldn't resist one more.

The kiss was gentle and then Jared stepped back. "Good

night, Jenny."

She couldn't see him walk away, but heard the click when he shut his bedroom door.

Smiling in delight, she closed her own door and skipped over to bed. She doubted she'd sleep much before dawn, but would much rather savor the kisses she'd received, recalling the delight each one had wrought.

* * *

Slowly Jenny came awake. It was after eight. Jenny looked over at the crib. Jamie still lay sleeping.

It was time to get up. Mrs. Giraux was expected for breakfast. Jared's parents would be arriving before lunch. She had a lot to do.

She hated to get up. Waking and feeding the baby hadn't made for a lot of sleep last night. She relished the early morning sounds. She could hear a bird chirp, hear some of the chatter from the sidewalk sweepers as they cleaned the square in preparation of the day.

It was growing warm, and soon she'd close her window to keep out the worst of the day's heat. But for now, she snuggled a moment longer. When she realized she could smell the coffee from the Café De Monde, she knew it was time to get going.

She was heating the bottle when the knock came on the door. Mrs. Giraux smiled at her when Jenny opened it.

"Come in. We're running a bit behind. I'm just going to feed Jenny and then will dash over to get our beignets," Jenny said breathlessly.

"Shall I come back later?" Mrs. Giraux asked.

"Of course not. Come in. If you like, you can feed her and I'll zip over and be back by the time she's finished eating."

"A perfect idea."

"Then come out on the balcony. I love feeding her there in the mornings. It's cool and she can look at the flowers."

In a few minutes Jenny had them settled.

"Jared's still asleep, I think. But if he comes down, tell him I started the coffee. It'll be done by the time I get back."

"Go on, we'll manage just fine, won't we, precious?" Mrs. Giraux spoke to the baby, her faded eyes lighting up when she looked at Jamie.

Jared had not come down by the time Jenny returned. Nor by the time she and Mrs. Giraux had finished breakfast. Nor by the time Jenny put Jamie down for her morning nap.

She was beginning to wonder if he was all right.

Tidying the apartment after Mrs. Giraux left, she brought in some blossoms from the balcony plants to fill her vase. The living room looked quite different from the night she'd arrived. Colorful and warm, it welcomed her every time she stepped in. She hoped Jared didn't mind. He hadn't said anything and if there was one thing she knew about him it was that he didn't hold back.

She was getting ready to go up to see if he was all right when she heard a knock on the door. Opening it, she came face-to-face with Jared's parents.

Chapter Nineteen

Surprised, Jenny glanced at her watch. Were they early? No, it was almost noon. Where was Jared?

"Hello," Jenny said brightly, wishing fervently Jared would show up. She'd met his mother at an open house when she'd come one time to see Patti at the school. But this was the first time she had met his father.

Introductions were quickly made as Jenny invited them in.

"Where's Jared?" Liz Montgomery asked. "And the baby?"

"Both are still sleeping, I think," Jenny said.

"I'm going up to check on him. He's probably still suffering from that explosion and all. I can't imagine why they let him out of the hospital so early. And why he didn't come home..." Liz's voice trailed away as she climbed the stairs.

Jenny smiled at Paul Montgomery. "Can I get you some coffee?"

"Be delighted. The boy's all right, isn't he?" he asked, following her into the kitchen.

Boy? Jenny hid a smile. Somehow the term didn't fit the Jared she knew.

She dumped the old coffee, rinsed the pot and reached for the can of ground coffee.

"Yes, he's okay. Getting better each day. I think the only

lingering injuries are his cracked ribs and the broken ankle."

Glad for something to do, Jenny began to measure the coffee. By the time the water began to trickle into the pot, Liz Montgomery joined them in the kitchen.

"He'll be down in a few minutes. I have to say he looks better than I thought he would. But I can still see the bruises. It just scares me to death to think of that explosion. He could have been killed like Jim."

"But he wasn't, Liz. Don't go fretting," Paul said.

With a frown at her husband, Liz Montgomery looked back at Jenny. "I peeked in to see the baby," she said with a dreamy smile. "She's fast asleep, but looks adorable. I can't wait to hold her."

"I expect she'll wake in another hour or so," Jenny murmured.

Was Jared going to tell his parents the truth about the baby?

How would they react to the news? To his plans for Jamie's future?

Liz nodded and looked out into the living room. "The apartment looks different from the last time I was here. Are those flowers on the balcony?" She walked away, examining things on her way to the opened French doors.

"I'll bring the coffee out when it's ready," Jenny said. In only a moment she was alone when Paul joined his wife on the balcony. Grateful for the respite, Jenny wondered how long it would be before Jared came downstairs. She didn't want to be the one to entertain his parents. They came to see him and Jaime, not her.

Hearing the sound of the cast on the stairs, she placed cups on a tray.

"There you are, dear," Liz hurried back, hovering around her son. "How're you feeling? Come sit down. Can I get you anything? Have you had breakfast? Of course not, if you just got up."

"I'm feeling fine, Mother. I told you upstairs I'm doing okay."

He sidestepped around her and into the kitchen, his gaze going immediately to Jenny. That slow, lazy smile started and she felt her heart catch.

"Good morning, you should have wakened me."

"Hi. You must have needed the rest to sleep in so late."

"Couldn't you sleep?" Liz asked, still hovering, full of motherly concern. "Didn't the doctor give you something for pain? We can call Dr. Rowland."

Jared shook his head, his eyes amused as he stared at Jenny, daring her to make a comment.

"I have the company doctor here in New Orleans, Mom. I'm doing fine."

"You don't look fine. And you slept so late. You haven't done that since you were a teenager."

Jenny hid a smile. Jared was a lucky man to have a mother so concerned for him. Taking pity on his growing impatience, she offered a diversion.

"The baby was up in the middle of the night. She kept us both up. Jared just needed to catch up on sleep," Jenny said, grateful the coffee had finished brewing. "Who wants coffee?"

"I can fix you some scrambled eggs," Liz offered, heading for the refrigerator. When she opened it she nodded. "At least you have more food than the last time I was here."

"No eggs, Mom. Coffee will do."

Liz glanced over her shoulder, slowly closing the

refrigerator door. She studied each in turn.

Handing the cups of coffee around Jenny gestured to the white bag still on the counter. "There are a few beignets left if anyone wants one. They're wonderful, one of the treats of living here—fresh every day." Jenny felt like she was making a commercial.

"Let me make you a regular breakfast" Liz said.

"Mom, we're going out to lunch as soon as the baby wakes I can wait until then to eat. Coffee will hold me," Jared said, taking a sip of the hot beverage.

"Which brings up the subject of your daughter. How could you not tell us about her impending arrival? I cannot believe a son of mine—"

"Mom. Wait a minute. Let's sit down so I can explain," Jared interrupted. He followed his mother into the living room.

Jenny followed and perched on the arm of the easy chair. She watched as Jared paced around the room. He moved well with the walking cast evidencing only a slight limp. But even injured, he had a restless energy that was hard to contain. The forced inactivity must be hard for him to bear.

His father leaned back on the sofa watching him. Liz sat on the edge as if ready to jump up if needed.

Jared looked at his parents, then at Jenny.

"There's no easy way to say this, Mom. And I didn't want to write you about it. We need to discuss it and keep it in the family."

She paled and reached for her husband's hand. "What? Were you more seriously injured than you told us?"

"No. It's not about me, Mom. It's the baby. Jamie's not mine."

"I don't understand. The letter you wrote to your sister said you were bringing home your baby," Liz said, clearly puzzled.

"Whose baby is it?" Paul asked.

"She is the daughter of a man I worked with. Both he and the baby's mother are dead. There was no one there to take care of her, so I brought her here figuring she ought to grow up in her father's country."

"What happened to her parents?" Paul persisted. "Why did you take on this infant? You don't want to get tied down with something like this, son. Think of the places you still want to see, the traveling ahead."

"Who was the mother? Why did you tell everyone she was yours? How did you get her out of the country and into this one?" Liz asked, clearly puzzled.

"The mother was a very nice Arab woman. She became ill after having the baby. When the father died, she had the birth certificate altered—listing me as father—which simplified getting Jamie into this country. And it will make it easier for me to arrange for her adoption."

"Adoption!"

"Smart move, son. You're in no position to care for a baby," Paul said.

"Why can't the father's family take care of her, if it's so important for her to be in the United States? Or the mother's family?" Liz asked.

Jared rubbed the back of his neck. "He didn't have any family. Nor did the mother."

He glanced at Jenny as if warning her not to contradict.

She shrugged. She wasn't going to contribute anything. These were his parents, he could tell them what he wished.

"So you volunteered to take on this baby?"

"To see she gets a good home."

"It's Jim Draydon's baby, isn't it? Good heavens, does Margaret know?" Liz guessed, leaning back and looking at her husband. "Oh dear, I can't believe it. You wouldn't do something like this for just anyone— it has to be Jim."

"Margaret hasn't a clue. That's the primary reason I've let everyone think the baby's mine," Jared said quickly. "And you can't tell anyone. Understand?"

"No," Liz said fretfully. "I don't understand any of it."

Jared sat on the sofa arm and began to explain the events to his mother. He could tell she didn't approve of his motives in claiming Jamie as his own. She grew angry with Jim and then concerned that Margaret would find out and be devastated.

"There's no way for her to ever find out unless one of us tells her," Jared insisted. "As far as the legal records are concerned, I'm her father. No one's going to question that if we give them no reason to do so."

"Well I certainly won't tell Margaret or the children. She adored Jim."

"As did those children. Seems to me a man has a responsibility to his family. Jim didn't live up to his," Paul said heavily.

"That's neither here nor there now, Dad. The fact is Jim is dead, and I see no reason for Margaret and the children to learn of what happened. Jamie's a pretty baby. I'll find her a good home and she'll be fine."

Liz looked at him for a long moment. "Why not keep her yourself? Jim was your best friend. I bet he would like you to raise his child."

Jared flicked a quick glance at Jenny. She smiled smugly.

Trust the women to band together.

"It's not practical, Mom. As soon as my ankle's healed, I'll be heading back."

"When are you going to give up living in foreign countries and come home? I don't understand you at all," she said. "What's wrong with Louisiana?"

"I'm not getting into that old discussion today," Jared said.

"Let the boy live his own life, Liz. He's free as a bird, going where he wants, doing what he wants. Wish I'd had the chance to see the world."

A soft cry on the monitor had Jenny jumping up. "That's Jamie. I'll get her up and be right back."

Jared watched her as she ran up the stairs. When he looked at his mother a second later, she was regarding him speculatively.

"What?"

"She's a pretty woman," Liz said slowly.

"She's beautiful and you know it. And funny, enthusiastic and takes great care of the baby. I was lucky Patti offered her the job," he said, hoping to diffuse any speculation on his mother's part.

"I hear a but," she said.

"Mom, as soon as I'm fit, I'm heading back. I'll get my attorney to find a home for the baby. Jenny will be back in Whitney before school starts. That's all. No buts—but nothing else, either."

Jared crossed to sink into the chair Jenny had vacated. He felt impatience rise. How long would she be?

"Has your attorney given you a time frame?" Paul asked.

"I haven't contacted him yet," Jared said, stretching out his legs.

"Why not? These things could take time. You don't want to hold up your return."

"There'll be time enough. I'm not going anywhere that soon. Jenny could always watch her even if I weren't here. She has until September before school starts, right?"

Jenny came down carrying Jamie. She'd dressed the baby in the lacy dress Mrs. Giraux had crocheted and tied a small pink ribbon in her hair.

"This is Jamie." She held her in her arms and crossed to Liz. The baby was fussing, but not yet crying.

"She's darling." Liz held out her hands and took the baby. "Paul, look, isn't she sweet?"

Liz looked at Jared. "I think you should consider keeping her, raising her yourself. She's Jim's child. If you had a child and we couldn't have cared for it, I think Jim would have raised that child for you."

Jared shook his head. "I'm in no position to be responsible for a baby."

"If you got married, your wife could watch the baby while you were in the field," Paul said.

Jenny glanced from one to another.

Backing up, she turned to the kitchen. She wanted no part in this discussion. Preparing a bottle, she tried to ignore the conversation in the other room, but it was clear Jared's parents thought he should get married and raise the baby. Even his father—though of course he thought the new wife should have the honor of caring for the child while Jared continued his nomadic existence. No wonder Jared felt as if he had to stay away. She wouldn't be happy with a father who constantly harped on leaving.

The points he made, however, were good. Jim had been a

close friend most of Jared's life. He probably did want Jared to raise his daughter.

What if Jared came around to their thinking? Would he offer marriage to some woman just to obtain a mother for the baby? Like Tad had tried for his sons?

Jenny felt cold. She knew Jared had no intentions of marrying. Not even to obtain a mother for Jamie. She knew they had no future together. And she would not let any daydreams interfere. She couldn't change his mind. She wouldn't even try any more.

And not for anything would she consider a marriage solely to become a mother, no matter how much she loved the baby.

She wanted love for herself. To be cherished for herself alone, not as a surrogate parent.

It'd be better if Jared found Jamie a happy home where both parents loved her and gave her the best they had.

And the sooner he did so, the sooner she could return home to Whitney. Remove herself from temptation, from the fantasy dreams that sometimes filled her night. Dreams that she and Jared fell in love. Dreams that they could build a future together.

Time to put an end to those fantasies once and for all.

Jenny brought the bottle back into the living room.

"I'll take her now. I know you want to go out for lunch," she said, reaching for Jamie.

"You're coming too," Jared said.

"No, I'm not." She met his gaze, tilting her chin firmly. "If you want to take Jamie, I'll feed her and get her ready. But your parents came to visit you, not me. You need to spend time with them."

Jared rose. "I expected you to accompany us."

Jenny smiled, though it didn't reach her eyes. She held firm to her new resolve. No time like the present to implement it.

"No, thank you anyway. Do you want to take Jamie, or not?"

"Not if you're not coming."

"We'd love to have you come with us," Liz said politely.

"Thank you, but you need to spend the time with your son. You can see Jamie this afternoon and evening. She doesn't sleep all the time—it just seems like it. And when she's awake, she has the sweetest disposition."

Jenny went out to the rocker and listened as Jared and his parents left for lunch. She suspected she and Jared would have spent the day quite differently if his parents had not arrived.

"But we can't be selfish, sweetie," she said to Jamie as the baby drank her milk. "We've had him since he arrived. He needs to spend some time with his parents, doesn't he? They haven't seen him in so long."

Jamie stared at Jenny as she chewed on the rubber nipple.

"Are you finished?" Jenny asked, moving the nipple around in her mouth, taking it out and skimming it over her lips. Jamie smiled.

"Oh, Jamie, you're smiling!"

Love washed through Jenny as the baby crinkled her face in a definite smile.

"What a cutie! I wish your daddy could see you." She stopped. She thought of Jared as Jamie's father. The baby belonged with him. Why couldn't he see that?

Anxious to share the news with someone, she hurried to Mrs. Giraux's door. Knocking, she waited impatiently for a response. None came. Maybe their neighbor had gone out. She was just turning to return to the apartment when the door opened a crack.

"Mrs. Giraux, are you all right?" Forgotten was the baby's smile at the sight of the older woman. Her hair was tousled and her cheeks flushed.

"I was lying down. I felt a bit under the weather this morning at breakfast, but thought it would pass. Instead, I'm feeling poorly now. A nap will set things to rights," she said, her voice sounding hoarse.

"Can I get you something?" Instinctively Jenny reached out to place her palm on the older woman's drawn face. She was burning up.

"Feels like you have a fever to me. Let me put the baby down and get you some aspirin."

"I don't want to be a bother."

"It's no bother. Go back and lie down, leave the door ajar. I'll be right back."

By the time Jenny heard Jared and his parents return, she was seriously worried about Mrs. Giraux.

Chapter Twenty

Jenny hurried to the landing between the apartments when she heard them on the stairs.

"Thank goodness, you're back," she said.

"What's wrong?" Jared asked as soon as he saw her.

"Mrs. Giraux is really sick. She has a fever and can't stop coughing. I've given her aspirin, but I think she should see a doctor. She didn't seem sick at breakfast. To become so ill so fast scares me. I can take her, but didn't want to expose the baby."

"We'll both take her. Do you have her doctor's number?"

"Yes. We called but he's gone this weekend. His service is trying to locate his backup. But I thought I'd take her to Urgent Care at the hospital," Jenny said.

"Want to take our car?" Paul asked. "It's not far."

"I can get mine.   I'd be more comfortable driving my own."

"I can take her," Paul offered.

"Thanks, but she knows me."

"We'll watch Jamie. Is she sleeping?" Liz asked. Jared opened the door to his apartment to ease the crowding on the landing.

"Yes, if you could feed her when she wakes, that would be

great," Jenny said, unhooking the baby monitor from her waist and handing it to Liz. "Jared knows where everything is and how much to feed her."

"I've raised two of my own and helped Patti when hers were small, I can manage," Liz said dryly. "You and Jared take care of his neighbor."

Jenny glanced at Jared. At his nod she felt a feeling of relief. She didn't want all the responsibility for getting the older woman to the hospital. What if she got worse?

"Thanks. If I get the car, can you get Mrs. Giraux downstairs in a few minutes? She'd never walk as far as where we parked. I'll drive out front and meet you two there."

"We'll manage," he said, stepping into his neighbor's apartment.

"I know she isn't your responsibility, but she's all alone," Jenny said, placing her hand on his arm.

"It's not that big a deal, Jenny. She helped us out by watching Jamie the other night. We'll reciprocate. Isn't that what neighbors are for?"

By nine that night Mrs. Giraux was back in her own bed. The doctors had diagnosed acute bronchitis, started her on antibiotics and recommended bed rest for several days. Jenny volunteered to stay with her.

"That will leave you alone with Jamie, can you manage?" she asked Jared after Mrs. Giraux was safely tucked in her bed.

"You're talking to the man who brought her all the way from the United Arab Emirates," he said loftily.

"I'm talking to the man who had flight attendants watching her most of the way," Jenny said tiredly.

"Ah, but look at all I've picked up since you've been with us." He reached out and massaged her shoulder.

"That relieves my mind."

"Hey," he said gently as he rubbed her shoulders. "We'll be fine. If I get in a bind, I'll come get you. You need some rest. You look exhausted."

"I am tired."

"Sleep tight, " he said, drawing her closer until she rested against his chest.

Jenny's arms came around his waist and she leaned against his strength. She'd love to remain just as they were all night. But his parents would be anxious to get to their hotel, and she needed to fix herself a place to sleep where she could hear Mrs. Giraux call out if she needed Jenny.

Jared tipped her face up and brushed his mouth across hers.

She smiled, then remembered her vow. Straightening, she stepped back. "It's getting late and your folks are still watching Jamie. Go on home. I'll be fine."

He hesitated, studying her closely. "Are you deliberately erecting some sort of barrier or am I imagining it?

Widening her eyes in surprise, Jenny shook her head. "I'm tired, and you could use a good night's rest as well. Go."

He didn't move for a long moment, then nodded.

"I'll see you in the morning."

"Take your parents out to brunch. I'll see how Mrs. G. is in the morning. If she can be left alone for a little while, I'll watch Jamie."

"We'll take her. You rest up and watch out for our neighbor."

Jenny walked him to the door, closing it softly when he stepped onto the landing. Our neighbor. Was Jared softening on his hands-off stance? He'd been kind and attentive to the older woman that evening. Solicitous. Maybe he'd find it wasn't all bad—being a neighbor.

Jenny felt at loose ends when she awoke the next morning with no baby to care for. She checked on Mrs. Giraux, pleased to notice the woman had slept during the night. Preparing her a light breakfast, Jenny listened for sounds from Jared's place. But the walls were thick. She heard nothing.

"You run along home, now, child. I'm feeling much better," Mrs. Giraux said when Jenny leaned over to pick up the empty breakfast tray a half hour later.

"I'll stay a bit longer. Maybe if you take a nap this morning, I'll dash over and take a quick shower."

"I'm fine. Feeling much better. That young doctor knew what he was talking about, I guess. And the medicine is already working. Run along now."

Jenny shook her head, smiling at the frail woman.

"I'll do these few dishes and then you and I can read the Sunday paper, how would you like that?"

"I don't want to be taking up your time. Jared will need you for the baby."

"Jared can manage fine. He's mobile now and used to taking care of her. I even got him to change her once so he knows how to handle that. The time together will be good for them."

"She is so precious. How can he not see that?"

"I'm hoping he'll fall for her so much he won't want her going anywhere. And I think he'd make a great father if he'd just get over the notion he isn't living if he isn't somewhere far from American shores. He talks to her when he thinks I'm not around. And plays patty-cake."

But more often than not, he left Jamie's care totally up to

her. Maybe a day together would help him see how well he could manage a baby.

When Mrs. Giraux drifted to sleep a few hours later, Jenny dashed to Jared's apartment to change her clothes.

It was empty.

For a moment Jenny felt a pang of loneliness. They'd done so much together over the last two weeks--just the three of them-- she felt left out now that he and Jamie were with his family.

"Nonsense. That's not your family. You're only working for Jared," she admonished herself as she climbed the stairs to her room.

She took her shower, dressed in a cool sundress and sandals, then returned to Mrs. Giraux's. At loose ends, she picked up the crochet sample Mrs. Giraux was using to teach her the craft. Her erratic stitches looked nothing like Mrs. G.'s neat, even ones. Would she ever be as skilled? Plodding away at it gave her something to do so she wouldn't go crazy missing Jared.

The knock on the door was soft. Rising, Jenny hurried to answer it.

"Hi." Jared stood there, Jamie in one arm, her head resting on his shoulder, and a big bouquet of flowers in the other hand.

"Hi yourself. Come in."

"These are for Mrs. Giraux. Is she feeling better?" he said, holding out the bouquet.

"She's napping now, but feeling better than she did last night. Did you enjoy your brunch?"

He nodded. "And Jamie was good as gold. Of course Mom held her the entire time. That could have something to do with it."

"Not so, Jamie's always good as gold, aren't you, sweetie? Come in and let's find a vase for these. Mrs. G. will love them."

"How long before she wakes up?"

"I don't know. Soon, I guess." Jenny rummaged through the various cupboards in the kitchen until she found a large crystal vase. Filling it with water, she arranged the bouquet, tilting her head as she studied the blossoms.

"This is nice of you," she said.

"News flash, I can be nice."

"I'll have to remember that in the future. Isn't Jamie sleepy?"

She glanced at the two of them, struck again by how right Jared looked holding the infant. Her heart melted another degree.

"I'll put her down soon." He rubbed his chin gently against the infant's curly dark hair, looking at Jenny with devilment in his gaze.

"My folks are gone for a while. Want to put Jaime down for her nap?"

"I better stay here in case Mrs. Giraux wakes up and needs something."

He looked at her as if picking up the change in her manner. "I thought she was feeling better. She's not capable of getting anything herself?"

"She shouldn't be up long enough to cook. Rest is the best thing for her."

"I didn't say leave and never come back," he said quietly.

"Well, I don't think I should right now," she said, fiddling with the flowers.

He reached out and caught her arm, turning her gently

until she faced him.

"Cut to the bottom line here, Jenny. What's going on?"

Jenny hesitated, wondering how to best put it. "Meeting your friends was fun. I enjoyed getting to know some of them. But the expectation was more than we are friends. Maybe it's time to reestablish the ground rules. I work for you. I'm here to take care of Jaime. But we want such different things out of life and I think as tempting as your kisses are, it would be better for me to make sure I don't get carried away in thinking more than can ever be."

"You know where I'm going."

She nodded. "And you know I'm heading back to Whitney when I leave at the end of the summer." She smiled, though she felt as if her face would crack. "I'm just saying I think we should back off a little. Or at least look at what we're doing a bit more. Take things slowly."

"Isn't that just like a woman, trying to analyze something to death!"

"Men usually like to analyze things," she replied lightly.

"So you're saying no?"

"Actually, I'm saying, I'd like to think about it a bit more."

Jared's smiled kicked up at that. He leaned over and kissed her again. Holding the baby cramped his style. He really wanted to pull her into his arms, so he could feel every sweet inch of her.

From her response, he knew she wasn't as indifferent as she was trying to make out. The question was, why was she feigning indifference to begin with?

He left after the kiss, taking Jamie home, hoping Jenny wouldn't be too long in following.

He'd spend the rest of the afternoon jotting more notes

about Jim's life.

He'd mentioned to his mother what he was doing and she had offered to dig out some of the pictures she had from when the two boys had been young and send them to him.

The project was turning out to be more complex than he'd anticipated. But why not? Jamie had no other way to know about her parents. And Jim had been a good friend for too long to ever forget. Jamie should know about her father.

He still had a hard time believing his friend was gone. Leaning back on the sofa, Jared let his mind roam, remembering the past. Jim had always been ready to start anything, go anywhere. His marriage hadn't slowed him down.

Thinking about families and choices, Jared realized that his father had chosen to live his life as he had. There'd been enough money for vacations over the years. Ample time to explore different countries, different cultures if he'd wanted. Even armchair explorations would have opened the world to his father.

But he had ignored the things available to him and chose instead to complain about the idealistic lifestyle he couldn't live.

Jim, in contrast, had done just as he pleased.

For the first time Jared wondered how hard that had been on Margaret and his children. How many Christmases had Jim missed with his family? How many birthdays? Despite all the grumbling from his father, he'd been there while Jared was growing up.

When the baby woke, he prepared her bottle and took her out onto the balcony as Jenny often did. Three weeks ago he was lying in a hospital bed, his experience with children limited to the occasional afternoon visits to his sister's house when he was in the States.

Now he felt like an old hand in caring for an infant. Amazing.

Even more amazing was the smile on Jamie's face.

He felt a kick in his heart. She was adorable.

"You're going to lose the suction on that nipple," he warned, intrigued with the way her face seemed to light up. Did she resemble Jim when she smiled?

As if she understood, she latched onto the nipple and drank for a long moment Then that smile appeared again—her eyes bright.

"So what's got you in such a good mood?" he asked, unable to take his gaze from her. She latched onto the nipple again. "Playing games, I think."

His heart ached for his friend. He'd been too young to die. Now he'd miss the delight in watching this child grow. In seeing how his other children turned out. Wasn't Tommy almost ten? Jim and Margaret had married as soon as Jim graduated from university and had their first baby within the year. Now they had two boys and a girl.

"Who are you talking to?" Jenny asked coming out onto the balcony.

"Jamie. She's smiling. Watch."

"I know. I saw it yesterday. Isn't she darling? That's why I went to Mrs. Giraux's yesterday, to show her off. Oh, Jamie, are you a happy girl?"

Jenny leaned over Jared's shoulder and smiled at the baby totally conscious of Jared only inches away. Without any effort she could turn her head and kiss him. Let her hands rest on his shoulders and savor his strength.

"You back for good?"

"Until later. Mrs. Giraux had some ladies from her church

stop by. They brought dinner, so I thought they should visit together. I'll go back over later and stay with her tonight."

"What about me and Jamie?" Jared asked in feigned distress. "We want Jenny here, don't we, Jamie?"

Jenny laughed and patted him on the shoulder, secretly savoring the connection. "You seem to be doing fine the two of you. Maybe you don't even need me anymore."

"Don't get any ideas."

Jenny walked to the railing and gazed over the square. "More tourists on the weekends."

"More in summer. In the winter the square's often deserted during the week."

She turned and leaned against the railing and watched Jared feeding Jamie. Jared's hair was dark, as was the baby's. He looked much more confident holding her than he had that day at the department store. When he put down the bottle and raised Jamie against his shoulder, Jenny smiled. She wished she could capture the picture they made for all time—the rugged engineer and the tiny delicate baby girl.

Jenny felt a shiver of foreboding. How much longer was this idyll setting going to last?

She wanted to snatch every minute and hold it close. Stop the steady tick of the clock. Keep everything just as it was this minute.

Jenny knew it was a futile wish.

Jared continued to heal. Many of his bruises had faded completely. His ribs rarely bothered him. He only had another week or two in the cast. Once his doctor declared him fit, he would take off.

And he held constant to his plan to place Jamie with another family.

As a summer job, this is the pits, Jenny thought suddenly. How could she have thought to get through it unscathed? She loved children. Her heart had not been love-proofed against this sweet baby.

Nor against the designated daddy.

The feelings that filled her had nothing to do with longevity or dreams of a future together. She knew Jared was leaving.

And when he did, he'd take her heart.

She loved him so strongly she was amazed he didn't recognize it. That the entire world didn't know.

The feelings she remembered for Tad seemed insignificant and paltry compared to what she now felt. She loved Jared's sense of honor, his laughter, and even the way he tried to hide his growing concern and involvement with his neighbor.

Not that she thought he was perfect. Far from it.

But he would be perfect for her.

If he only wanted to build a family, share his life with one person. Put down roots. Love her.

Because no matter what, Jenny was still determined to find a family for herself. She wanted ties and roots and traditions and commitments and responsibilities. She yearned for them. And for a feeling of belonging to someone, somewhere, forever. A commitment so strong that nothing could ever sever the ties of loyalty and love.

So she'd bid Jared goodbye when he left, forget him as soon as she was able and continue her search for a family of her own. It would hurt—as would saying farewell to Jamie.

Suddenly she couldn't take any more. She hurried into the apartment, longing to escape her thoughts— and the two people in the world who had come to mean everything to her.

Chapter Twenty-One

She'd go for a walk, she thought. Get away until she could get her tumbling emotions under control.

Jared could manage Jamie and she could use the time to herself.

Before she could leave, there was a knock on the door.

"Jared, are you expecting anyone?" she called as she went to answer it.

"No."

Opening the door, Jenny saw a slender young woman she didn't know.

The woman seemed surprised to see her. "Miss Stratford?"

"Yes? I'm sorry, I don't recognize you."

"You wouldn't. I'm Margaret Draydon. My younger son was in Mrs. Webb's first grade last year. I've requested my daughter be placed in your class this fall. I didn't like the way Mrs. Webb handled her students."

Margaret Draydon, Jim's widow. Jenny swallowed.

All she could think of was the baby on the balcony.

"It's nice to meet you. I'll look forward to having your daughter in my class."

"I didn't expect you here. Isn't this Jared Montgomery's place?" Margaret asked.

"It is. Come in, Jared's here."

Jenny turned when she closed the door and saw Jared had already come into the living room, still carrying Jamie.

"Margaret," he said, crossing to give her a kiss on the cheek.

"I'm sorry to show up unannounced," Margaret said rushing into a speech. "But Mama said she'd watch the children so I just drove down. This way I can return. Can I talk to you now?" She seemed to see the baby for the first time.

"Oh, your baby. Your mother told me about her a few weeks ago. What a surprise. I never saw you as the family type."

"Patti hired Jenny to watch her until—" He met Jenny's gaze and shrugged. "For the summer. Till I can manage on my own. Sit down. Can I get you anything?"

Margaret shook her head.

Jenny took Jamie. "I'll change her and keep her upstairs so you two can talk."

Jared wanted to ask her to stay, but he knew Margaret hadn't driven from Whitney to talk in front of a stranger. When she made no comment, he knew he had to face this alone.

When Jenny was gone, Margaret tried to smile. "It's been a long time, Jared. How are you doing? Your mother's been so worried. I was sorry to hear you'd been injured."

Her eyes welled with tears. She bit her lower lip. "I need to talk to you about Jim."

"I know. I was going to see you before I returned to the site. I don't have the words to make it better. I can't believe he's gone. Come over and sit down."

Jared sat beside her on the sofa and stretched out his legs, resting his broken ankle on the coffee table.

"I'm almost back to normal. As soon as the ankle heals, I'll be back in the field. But I will swing by Whitney to see you and the kids."

"What about your daughter? Surely you aren't taking her back there, too? Or will your parents watch her? I understand her mother's dead. I'm so sorry."

He nodded. "The baby'll stay here in America."

He wasn't going into details with Margaret. The disapproval from Jenny, Mrs. Giraux and his mother was enough. He'd be gone by the time others learned of Jamie's adoption. Let them think what they would.

"I'm sorry I couldn't make the funeral," he said as the silence stretched out.

Margaret nodded. "I didn't expect it. You were still in the hospital. It was a nice service. He's buried near his parents."

She played with the strap of her handbag, obviously nervous.

Jared nodded. The next time he went to Whitney, he'd have to visit the cemetery and say goodbye to his old friend.

"You wanted to talk about Jim?" Jared said at last.

She looked at him nervously and tried to smile. "I guess I wanted closure or something. How was he this last year? Was he happy? Did he enjoy life? You know he hadn't been home for a visit in almost a year. Normally he came back every six months. But he didn't come last winter when he'd been scheduled. I, uh, wondered if things had been going well or badly for him."

"He liked the work."

Jared roiled against the fate that put him in this situation. He knew his friend had been so taken with Sohany he hadn't taken his normal leave in the States. What excuse had he given his wife?

"He didn't write often." Margaret smiled sadly. "He never did. Email was sporadic. We'd see him almost every week on Skype, but that's not the same as being home. The kids don't even seem to miss him. Isn't that a terrible legacy to leave? But you know he was always gone more than he was home."

She looked as if she was about to cry.

Jared considered calling Jenny. She could help if Margaret began to cry, he didn't have a clue about what to do with a weeping woman.

"He loved you and the children," Jared said, feeling like he was floundering. "The pay is so extraordinarily good, he took the assignments to provide for you all."

She nodded, gazing out through the opened French doors.

"You were his closest friend, so I thought I should tell you in person."

She took a breath and looked at Jared. "I'm getting married again. Soon. At Thanksgiving."

"What?" That was the last thing Jared expected.

"It'll seem sudden to most, I know. But it's not. Chuck Lymack and I have been seeing each other for a time. It's been hard to be virtually a single parent for all these years. Jim was only home for a few weeks at a time and then gone for months. I really wanted him to come home this past winter. I was going to ask for a divorce. But he kept postponing his rotation and it wasn't something I wanted to discuss by letter or on Skype. I thought he'd be sure to come the next month or the next. Only, he never did."

Jared stared at her. "You were going to divorce him?"

Margaret nodded. "He was never there for me, Jared. A woman wants a mate to be a part of her life, not just a source of money sent each month. His children deserve to have a father. A full-time father. Someone who will attend school functions, show them how to be part of a couple, teach them how to grow up and become good adults."

"I'm not arguing with you, Margaret. You just caught me by surprise."

"I know. I don't know quite why I came. To hear that he wouldn't have minded a divorce, I guess. To hear that he liked the single life or something. To find out why he wanted to be there in the desert rather than home with me and his children."

Jared thought of Sohany and Jamie. Had Margaret told Jim, what would he have done? Married Sohany, he bet. Jim said he loved her. She'd been born and raised in Abu Dhabi and wouldn't have minded the site accommodations in the least. It would have changed everything with her family as well.

"He would have been all right with it," Jared said. He didn't want to say more.

"I think so, too. Anyway, it seems so soon after his death and all. But Chuck and I have been discussing this for months. If Jim had come home as he had originally planned, the divorce would have been underway and no one would think it odd I'm marrying so soon."

"Do the children like Chuck?"

"They adore him. He's great with them, loves them to death. He takes the boys to ball games and Lisbeth to the movies. Imagine a grown man sitting through a little girl's choice of movie. He makes all our lives special, Jared."

"I'm glad for you."

"I wanted your approval. You knew Jim better than anyone in the world. If you think it's okay, I'll feel— less guilty, I guess. We never should have married. Jim didn't want to settle down any more than you do. A long-distance marriage is too hard. And it wasn't fair to me or the children."

"He loved you and the kids."

"I know. In his way he did. But he yearned to be free more than he wanted to live with us. I just wonder what he found in the Middle East that couldn't be found here."

Jared heard the echo of Jenny's question in Margaret's comment. Looking around the colorfully decorated living room, baby things here and there, the hastily stacked notes about Jim and Sohany, the beginning crochet project, the files from work, he questioned it himself.

This was a home. His flat in Abu Dhabi was merely a place to sleep and change his clothes.

When had the change happened?

A flare of panic touched. He had to get out before he became used to this soft life. Before he began to think that he wanted something different, and before he started to believe that that something included Jenny and Jamie. He had his life set and no temporary play family was going to change it!

"Go home, Margaret and marry your Chuck. Jim would never have wanted you to be alone after he died."

"Not that he cared that much when he was alive," she grumbled. "Sorry, I'm still mad at him for dying. It's hard to get through the day sometimes. I loved him so much when we were younger. But it's gone, now."

She looked at Jared.

"If you ever fall in love, stay with her. Or let her go and move on. Don't be an absent husband or father."

"I don't think that will ever apply, but I'll keep it in mind," he said. It was time he got things underway once he was fit again.

"So tell me about where he lived and what the two of you did for entertainment," Margaret said, relaxing for the first time as she waited to hear about the last months of her husband's life.

It was late by the time Margaret left. Jared urged her to stay overnight in New Orleans before heading home, but she said she was too keyed up to sleep so might as well drive back to Whitney.

The relief when he shut the door behind her was almost tangible. She didn't suspect anything amiss with Jim's life, still remained ignorant about Jamie's parentage. And she seemed happier than when she'd arrived.

"Jenny?" he called up the stairs.

She came to the top a second later.

"She's gone."

Descending, she studied his face. "How did it go?"

When she reached the bottom, he drew her into his arms and hugged her, resting his cheek against her hair, drawing comfort.

"Better in one sense then I expected, worse in another. She was going to ask Jim for a divorce the next time he came home."

"Oh, wow."

"Yeah, I know."

"Then he could have married Sohany," she said softly.

Jared nodded.

"It's all so tragic."

Jenny leaned against him, making no move to draw away. He relished the feel of her arms around him, the contentment he felt.

The first meeting with Margaret was over. They wouldn't

see each other often in the future. Her life would take a different direction.

And she need never discover Jim's indiscretion.

"I bet you're hungry," he said. "I didn't expect her to stay so long."

"I can fix something quick. Then I need to go check Mrs. Giraux."

Mrs. Giraux was already tucked in bed. She had been tired after her friends' visit and insisted Jenny didn't need to stay. Making sure she had the phone handy and Jared's number as well as her cell number, Jenny bid her goodnight.

Jared was sitting on the balcony when she entered the apartment. The evening was balmy, a slight breeze from the river keeping things cool. She joined him, taking the rocking chair.

"It's relaxing to sit out after dark," she murmured.

"I like listening to the sounds, and the music. I wish only one place came through loud and clear instead of the music mixing," he said. "How's Mrs. G?"

"Already in bed. She seemed better earlier in the day. I hope her friends visiting wasn't too much."

"Probably much appreciated," he murmured.

Chapter Twenty-Two

By early afternoon, Jenny was ready for a nap. She and Jared had stayed up on the balcony until late. Then she'd been up early to take care of the baby. She'd washed a load of laundry and visited with Mrs. Giraux.

Pleased to see the elderly woman was much improved, she let herself be persuaded that her neighbor could manage fine on her own until dinnertime. Since Jamie was napping, maybe she could find some down time herself.

Jared was on the phone when she entered the apartment. Waving, she didn't stop, but crossed straight to the stairs and quickly went to her room. Peeking at Jamie, Jenny was pleased the baby was sleeping soundly. Without wasting any motion, Jenny slipped off her sandals and lay down on her bed. Her body ached, she was so tired. In only moments she was fast asleep.

When she awoke, the room was empty. Jared must have taken Jamie to let her sleep longer. She smiled. The nap helped. She felt full of energy.

Descending the steps, Jenny almost laughed to see Jared on the floor near the infant seat. He was typing on his laptop while Jamie seemed content to sit near him, her eyes watching his every move.

"Thanks for letting me sleep," Jenny said.

He looked up, holding her gaze for a long moment. Nodding, he said, "Obviously you needed it. I checked on Mrs. Giraux this afternoon. She's up, though still feeling weak and shaky."

"I hope she's not trying too much too soon."

Jenny wandered over and perched on the edge of the coffee table.

"What are you doing?"

"Trying to finish up this biography of Jim," he said, his eyes on the screen. "Sohany's sister sent some photographs. They came today." A couple clicks and a picture of a young girl appeared.

Jared clicked again and there was another picture. They went through the remaining few.

"Jamie's mother was very pretty, wasn't she? Is this one with Jim?" She pointed to the last one showing--a couple grinning at each other.

"Yes."

"That'll be nice for Jamie to have, one of her parents together."

"I called my attorney this afternoon," Jared said, not looking at her.

Jenny's gaze flew to him. He stared at the computer. Swallowing hard, she tried to ignore the clutch in her heart.

"About Jamie?" she asked, amazed she sounded almost normal.

He nodded.

Her gaze moved to the baby. Jamie was happily kicking her little legs, watching Jared. She was so full of life and joy. Jenny felt a sting of tears. This precious baby.

How could Jared not want to raise his friend's child?

"What did he say?" she asked, pleased her voice didn't break.

It was only her heart breaking.

Without volition, she remembered the aching days at the Home when she had so hoped a family would want her. Even today, she still longed for someone to care about her, worry if she was late getting home, share good times and bad.

"He'll get back to me. He has some contacts. Infants are highly desirable, he said. There's a good organization here in town that has high standards. It might be the best place to screen potential parents."

Jenny remained silent. There was nothing to say. Her throat ached holding back tears.

"It's time," Jared said. "I'll be ready to leave soon and need this taken care of before heading back to the Middle East."

He looked at her at last.

Jenny refused to meet his eyes. She watched Jamie, trying to imprint every detail of the baby on her mind. How long would it take someone to come forward to adopt her?

Not long, was her guess. Families liked babies. She remembered that from growing up. Everyone wanted an infant. No one wanted a troublesome, lonely, frightened child.

"It's not like you didn't know I was going to do this all along." His tone was sharp.

She looked at him then. "Yes, I knew it. I have never liked the idea. I've made no bones about that."

Jenny rose and picked up Jamie, holding her close, relishing the sweet baby scent, the soft squirming body. "We're going to Mrs. Giraux's," she said, turning and heading for the door.

"Jenny!"

Ignoring him, she hurried to the opposite door on the landing and rapped quickly.

Mrs. Giraux opened it. She wore a soft cotton robe and her hair had been brushed. There was a bit of color in her cheeks. But she looked older than she had a few days ago. Jenny felt a pang at the sight of her.

"We came to visit," she said, trying to smile.

"Come in. I'm delighted to see you both. Should you bring the baby? The doctor said I'm not contagious, but no sense taking any chances."

"He called the attorney," Jenny blurted out as the door closed behind her cutting off the sound of Jared calling her again.

"Oh dear." Mrs. Giraux looked dismayed. "I truly didn't believe he meant to do that. He would make a wonderful father."

"I think so, too. If he would only consider it. But he's got this notion in his head and nothing will budge it. He's going back, you know."

"Sit down, dear. Can I get you something?"

"Oh, Mrs. Giraux. You sit down and I'll get us both some tea. I came to see if you needed anything."

Jenny pulled one of Mrs. Giraux's soft crocheted afghans off the sofa and placed Jamie on it in the center of the living room floor. She hurried into the kitchen feeling as at home there as in Jared's apartment. Returning in only a minute, she handed Mrs. Giraux a glass of iced tea, placed her glass on the coaster, and sat on the floor next to Jamie, tickling her, brushing her fingertips over her soft skin.

"He came to see me earlier. Never mentioned a word,"

Mrs. Giraux said. "First time he's come to see me since he moved in. He wanted to make sure I was okay. To offer to get me anything I needed."

"He's been over a couple of times," Jenny said.

"Ah, but you've always been here those other times. He'd come to see you then. Today was for me. I'll miss you both when you're gone," she said with a sad smile. "It's quiet here when the apartment next door is empty."

"You'll have to come visit me in Whitney. I can come get you, or you could take the bus up. It's not very exciting, but it is a pretty town. And you can teach me more crochet patterns."

"You know, I think I would like that. I haven't been anywhere in a long time."

"We'll plan on it," Jenny said, trying to ignore the ache in her heart. First Jamie, then Jared. Both would be gone from her life soon.

She was not ready.

Jared studied the picture of Jim and Sohany. He remembered when it'd been taken—at the picnic they'd all gone on last New Year's Day. They'd spent the entire holiday together and he'd snapped the photograph with Sohany's camera. For a long time he looked at his friend's image.

"You left me one heck of a mess," he said. "But I'm doing the best I can. You know neither of us was cut out for this kind of life—stuck in one place, suffocated with ties and responsibilities. We were born to be free, to roam the earth, bring in oil."

The silence echoed with reproach, with regret.

"I tried it once, with Andrea. Look at what you and

Margaret had. She was going to divorce you. You were planning to leave Sohany. Men like us should never tangle with women."

Contemplating the picture another minute, Jared frowned.

"That's what you meant, wasn't it, when you asked me to watch out for your baby? To see she and Sohany were all right when you returned to the States?"

Doubt crept in.

Jim certainly had not expected him to raise his child. He knew Jared.

He couldn't have meant—

Jared slammed the tcp down on the computer and struggled to rise. Tomorrow he'd call his doctor and get an appointment for a new set of X-rays. His ankle hadn't bothered him in several days. Maybe it was healed.

He walked out onto the balcony. Restless energy, frustration, anger played within. He glared at the flowers, wanting to smash the pots on the street. He wasn't a man to have flowers around. He uttered an expletive under his breath. Jenny could take them home with her when she left. He wasn't going to be around long enough to keep them alive.

Swinging around, he glanced into the living room—warm and welcoming and lived in. For a long moment Jared surveyed every detail, every splash of color, every hint of domesticity. Flowers on the table, prints on the walls, braided rugs on the floor. Signs of Jenny and Jamie and himself.

The familiar feelings of claustrophobia began. Jared strode through the room and to the front door. No longer needing cane or crutches, he walked down the stairs and out into the late afternoon heat. He was footloose and fancy-free. No ties. He needed to remember that. In a few days, a week or two at the most, he'd be back where he belonged.

And Jenny Stratford would be nothing but a pleasant memory.

He started walking toward the bar he and Jim had always frequented when in town. Entering a few minutes later, Jared hesitated, looking around. He knew no one.

And without Jim, it was just another place to buy a drink. He turned and walked back outside and headed for the river. His cast didn't hinder his progress. Or if it did, he didn't notice. He'd clear his head before returning to the apartment. It wasn't as if she hadn't known what he planned. He'd told her often enough.

But the hint of tears in her eyes had hit him like a punch to the heart. He'd give her time to get over it, then return. If she wanted to talk, then he guessed he could discuss it once more. Not that he needed to justify his actions.

When Jared returned to the apartment, it was late. Jenny had left a lamp burning in the living room, but had obviously already retired. He missed her being there, missed her smile, her quiet voice.

That night set the tone for the next two days.

Jared was almost amused by the ways she found to avoid him. Or he would have been amused if it hadn't frustrated him so much.

She carried the baby everywhere. When they went for a walk, he was not invited. When they spent endless hours at the apartment next door, he was excluded. If he didn't know for certain that Mrs. Giraux was recovering, he'd think her at death's door.

He'd knocked one day, but was not invited in. Mrs. Giraux stood firmly in the doorway and demanded to know what he wanted. Old, frail and recovering from an illness not withstanding, she'd stood there like a defending angel. If he hadn't been so annoyed, he might have found it humorous.

Jenny cooked his meals. He couldn't fault her work performance.

But the joy was gone.

His mother sent pictures of Jared and Jim as boys. Jenny unbent long enough to look at them, with Jared explaining where each one had been taken. For that moment he felt the warmth she normally spread like sunshine. For several minutes the icy distance she'd maintained since he told her of the call dissipated.

But as soon as they were finished, she rose and almost ran up the stairs.

"How long are you going to act that way?" Jared murmured, gathering the photographs together and placing them in the now bulging envelope. He withdrew the written notes. Some of it was in Jenny's hand, other print outs from the computer. He was glad this would be going with the baby.

Writing it had brought him closer to his friend. They'd shared good times and bad together since they'd been in second grade. The aching pain of loss hadn't diminished. At least he had good memories.

When the phone rang Thursday morning, Jared picked it up. Jenny came from the balcony and stood there, staring at him, reproach shining in her eyes.

He kept his eyes on hers as he spoke. It was Arthur.

"Well?" she asked when he hung up.

"Arthur's arranged for the agency to take her. They have

several couples on the waiting list and he said Jamie will likely find a home within weeks."

Jenny said nothing, but her heart froze.

"If I go in today, Arthur said I can finalize all the paperwork and then bring the baby to him as early as tomorrow. The agency offers foster care until the adoption can be put through."

Jenny swallowed hard. "Tomorrow?" she said softly.

"As early as tomorrow. I could wait until next week, I guess," Jared reiterated, wishing he could erase the stricken look from her face.

"Or you could keep her until the adoptive parents are selected. How long will that take?"

He ran his fingers through his hair. "It doesn't matter. I have an appointment with the doctor on Monday. If the X-rays look good, the cast comes off. I can be released for desk duty at least, if not full field duty immediately."

"Well it looks like everything is going just how you wanted. Timing's great," she said bitterly.

He stepped closer, wanting to pull her into his arms, hold her, feel her soft body against his. Smell that delicious fragrance that was Jenny. He wanted her to want to be with him, but ever since that first call to Arthur, she'd treated him like he had leprosy.

He stopped a few feet away searching for some sign she would be receptive.

"I'll be going as soon as she's gone," Jenny said, holding her head high.

He wanted to protest.

Yes, of course she would. He'd hired her to watch Jamie. With the baby gone, why would Jenny stay?

"I'd like to see you next time I'm here. I get leave every six months or so," he said. Maybe if it wasn't a permanent split it would ease things.

The thought of leaving should make him happier. Instead, he ached at the expression on her face.

"I don't think there's any reason for that, Jared. When Jamie's gone, any reason for our seeing each other ends."

So much for believing there was something between them.

"Stay, just until I go," he urged.

She shook her head. "No."

"What we have is special. I'm not the only one to feel that, am I?"

"We don't have anything. You were attracted to me, I was to you. We acted on that attraction. Now it's time to go our separate ways. I'm certainly not going to sit home for six months or longer and hope you show up someday."

He rubbed his hand around the back of his neck in frustration. "I'm not asking you to sit around waiting for me. But if you're available when I get back, what's the harm in dinner out or something?"

Jenny stared at him for a long moment. "If you can't see the harm, then there's no sense talking about it"

She turned and went back out onto the balcony. He saw her sit in the rocker, head high, back ramrod straight.

He knew she was upset about Jamie, though her earlier comment was the first she'd made concerning his plans since he'd told her about the initial call to Arthur. To give her credit she hadn't nagged at him these last few days to change his mind.

Andrea would have. She'd have been at him night and day.

Jenny is nothing like Andrea, a voice inside reminded him.

As if he needed reminding.

He'd never felt for Andrea what he felt for Jenny. With Jenny.

Once Jamie was settled, maybe he could talk to her, get her to at least understand his side of things even if she couldn't agree with it. But first things first. He'd meet his attorney, sign the necessary papers this afternoon and make his decision on when to turn Jamie over to the adoption agency.

Jenny knew time moved at the same pace through eternity, but it seemed as if it dragged that afternoon. She held Jamie long after the baby fell asleep, reluctant to give her up for a minute.

"Don't you worry, sweetie," she said softly to the sleeping infant "whoever raises you will love you to death. You'll be cared for and cherished. And when you're older, you can see what your mama and daddy looked like. And know that they loved you."

At least Jared had given her that much.

When she heard the door open, she wanted to slam it shut keeping Jared and his news outside.

He came straight to the balcony. Looking at the baby, his gaze then moved to meet Jenny's.

"Well?" she asked, hoping against hope something had come up, something to make the transaction impossible.

"I'm to take her to Arthur's office tomorrow morning. As soon as she's in custody of the agency, they'll start proceedings to place her."

Jenny absorbed the news.

"There's no reason the prospective family can't take care of her pending the finalization of the paper work."

Jenny remained silent.

"The agency representative said they'd make sure the information about Jamie's parents went with her. That the adoptive parents would share it with her when she's older. I told them that Jim and Sohany had loved each other very much, but there were reasons they couldn't marry right away and then they died before they could. But I didn't say he was married to someone else."

"Jamie will like knowing that when she grows up," Jenny said slowly.

She thought she'd feel pain at the parting. But she felt numb. Gazing over the square, she let her mind drift— remembering the first night she'd met Jared. How noble she'd first thought him for taking his friend's baby. And how she'd fooled herself into thinking he was growing to love Jamie, and would come to the point where he wouldn't want to give the baby up.

Or give her up. She wanted him to tell her he couldn't live without her. That these weeks together meant more to him than anything he could ever find in the Middle East or any other spot in the world.

That he loved her.

That he wanted to build a life together and never let her go.

She loved him so much she ached. And he only thought about returning to the desert sands of the Middle East.

Get a grip, she admonished herself. He'd never deceived her. He'd been up-front every inch of the way. It was her own dreams that clouded things. He was leaving. And it was time she did as well.

Rising, Jenny put the rocker between them. "I'll go pack Jamie's clothes. Will they take any of the furniture?"

"No. I'll have Phil or Harry ask at the office if anyone needs it. Otherwise, I'll call one of the local charities."

A month ago she had not known this man. Now she had difficulty imagining how her life would unfold without him in it. Maybe things would look different in Whitney.

Funny, she had fled there to escape the gossip about her broken engagement. Now it had become her refuge, a sanctuary. She'd return home, start plans for the new school year. And do her best to put Jared Montgomery as far from her thoughts as she could.

Somewhere there was a man for her.

Somewhere, sometime she'd find the family she was searching for.

But it wasn't here and Jared Montgomery was no longer in the running.

Jared awoke the next morning to Jamie's frantic cries. Groggily, he rose and pulled on the shorts he'd been wearing. He couldn't wait to get the cast off his leg. Why wasn't Jenny getting the baby? Was she in the shower and couldn't hear her?

He pushed open the door to the second bedroom and crossed to pick up the baby. Only then did it register—the room looked vacant. Two small suitcases stood by the door— Jamie's clothes. The bed had been stripped. The spread and pillows stacked at the head. Opening the closet door, he saw it was empty. He yanked open the top dresser drawer—empty.

He walked down the stairs, a sinking in his gut. The living room looked lifeless and deserted. Gone were the prints from the wall. The end table was barren. Dark hardwood floors echoed as he walked, the colorful braided rugs had vanished.

For a moment he stared. This was the way his apartment used to look. It had never bothered him in the past.

But today—today it looked hollow and lifeless.

He looked on the balcony. She'd taken the colorful plants. Only the rocker sat in forlorn isolation.

Jenny was gone.

Jamie cried harder.

Jared placed her in the infant carrier and hurried to prepare her bottle.

"She left," he said to the baby once the cries had been silenced by milk. "Without saying goodbye. At least to me. Maybe she told you goodbye."

He rocked the infant and tried to ignore the void Jenny's going had created.

In a few hours he'd take Jamie to Arthur's office— the first step to locating new parents for her. Then he just needed clearance from his doctor and he could return to the life he'd known before the explosion. Carefree, no responsibilities, no ties.

There was a knock on the door. Had she returned? Forgotten something? Had second thoughts?

Jared hurried to open it.

"I came as soon as I read her note. Can I help?" Mrs. Giraux held out a folded sheet of paper.

"Come in. I'm feeding Jamie now. But if you wouldn't mind dressing her, that would be a help. Jenny left out the crocheted dress you made her." He tried a smile. "Guess she wanted the baby to look her best."

"Let me finish feeding her. I'm going to miss her so much. You can read the note if you wish."

Jared handed her the baby and took the folded paper.

"Mrs. G.: I'm heading for home. Jared's taking Jamie to the adoption agency in the morning. He no longer needs me, and I'm not one

for goodbyes.

Don't forget you promised to pay me a visit. I'll call you next week and we'll arrange a date. Thanks for teaching me to crochet, and for all the wonderful stories of old New Orleans.

Love, Jenny"

He no longer needs me, he reread. For the first time, he wondered if that was true.

Mrs. Giraux helped him prepare Jamie to leave. She carried the baby's small suitcases down to the cab, kissed her gently. Looking at Jared with tears in her eyes, she patted his arm as he prepared to climb into the cab.

"Just make sure you know what you're doing," she said.

Of course he knew what he was doing. The best he could for his friend's baby.

The driver pulled away from the curb, heading toward Arthur Perkin's office. Jamie sat in the infant carrier next to Jared, her arms waving. The crochet dress was fancy, as was the ribbon Mrs. Giraux had affixed in her hair. She was a darling baby. Anyone would love her, he thought with satisfaction. She'd have a good life with a couple who would love and cherish her.

"Right, Jamie?" he said softly. She looked at Jared with her wide brown eyes—and smiled.

Chapter Twenty-Three

Jenny didn't care that she'd taken the coward's way out and slipped away in the middle of the night. Actually, early morning—not that it mattered. She was well on the way to Whitney by the time Jamie would cry for her bottle.

Jared could cope for a few hours. And she'd left the message for Mrs. Giraux. The woman adored the baby, she'd make sure she was taken care of. She could get her dressed and even ride with Jared if she wanted to. Which is something Jenny couldn't face. She could not tell that precious baby goodbye and turn her over to some agency.

By the time she reached home, Jenny had a splitting headache. From holding back the tears, she knew. She unpacked as much as she could from the car, taking the plants first. They'd die in the heat otherwise. Leaving several nonperishable items for later, she fixed herself a light lunch. Then promptly burst into the long held back tears.

Confused as to whether she missed Jared or Jamie more, she went to her room to lie down. She hadn't slept last night. Nor could she sleep now.

Thoughts jumbled in her mind. Feelings swept through her, longings for Jared to hold her and tell her everything would be all right.

Only she'd burned that bridge, leaving him like that.

"It was the only way," she said to the ceiling, rubbing the ache in her heart. "He'll be leaving in another couple of days. I just left first."

Still, hope died hard. She had so fervently wished that something would happen, something to change his mind.

But there was no miracle. No vast sweeping change from on high that convinced him living in Louisiana was the best thing in the world.

The lure of foreign places and adventure called.

And Jenny Stratford, once again, wasn't enough.

Dashing the tears away, she sat up.

She was too enough. Maybe not for him, but for someone. And she wasn't going to find her perfect life's partner moping in her room.

By Saturday afternoon she'd gone an entire hour without thinking about Jared. Progress, she affirmed. She cleaned her apartment from top to bottom. Placing her purchases from New Orleans in various locations in her place, she was reminded of Jared with every item she unpacked. She remembered his odd look when he first spotted the silk cover for the end tables. His wary study of the colorful painting she'd hung over his sofa. His sitting on the braided rugs with Jamie.

She stared at her new things for a long moment, almost able to smell the fragrance of coffee from the Café du Monde, almost able to hear the jazz music filtering in from Preservation Hall. Taking a deep breath, Jenny tried to blank out the ache in her heart.

She'd spent a few weeks living in New Orleans. She should be grateful for that.

But it was hard to forget Jared.

Impossible so soon.

Sunday she went to church, staying afterwards for the fellowship hour, mingling with friends, meeting a few newcomers. Filling the hour with conversation and laughter—and delaying the return to her empty apartment.

Monday she went swimming at the country club as a guest of Suzie Taylor—one of her longtime friends. There Jenny encountered several students she'd taught over the past two years with their mothers.

Maybe she didn't have that family yet but she had a respective place in the community, and was valued. She enjoyed lunch with Suzie, lazing around the pool, and playing with some of the children.

Tuesday she ran into Tad. Their meeting began awkwardly, but after a few words, Jenny grew at ease. There was no animosity left on her part. And, more importantly--no regrets. Getting to know Jared proved to her Tad had never been the right man for her.

When he asked how she was doing, she explained where she'd been. When she asked after his boys, he eagerly talked about them. She felt better about their situation when he apologized for trying to marry her for the sake of his sons.

"Maybe we could still see each other?" he asked hopefully.

Jenny shook her head. "No, not like that. But if Simon is in my class next year, I'll see you at parent-teacher conference."

Later that afternoon a knock sounded at Jenny's door.

Jenny threw it open. Stunned, she stared at the rocking chair that gently moved to and fro in the doorway.

"You forgot that," Jared said.

"Jared," she said softly.

Eagerly her gaze roamed over him, trying to commit every feature to memory. His cast was gone. His khaki slacks encased long legs. The dark blue pullover shirt lovingly followed the sculpted lines of his muscles. His hair had been trimmed— probably in preparation for his departure. The bruises were gone.

For a second she was transported back to that night when she'd first seen him struggling up the steps. Now she knew him better.

Her heart rate was out of control. Wiping her damp palms on her shorts, she debated what to do. Slam the door in his face or let him in.

After a long moment, she stepped aside.

"Come in."

Had he come to tell her goodbye? She should have left him a note like she had Mrs. G.

He lifted the rocker effortlessly and stepped inside. Pausing a moment, he looked around the room. Spotting an open space, he crossed the room and set the rocker down.

"I couldn't fit it in the car," she said nervously. Slowly closing the door, she leaned against it, watching him warily. He could have kept the rocking chair. Donated it with the rest of the baby furnishings.

He studied the familiar painting newly hung over her sofa. Slowly turned around the room, he took in the various things she'd purchased in New Orleans, the other decorations that defined her living room, finally letting his gaze move to her.

"You left rather abruptly," he said mildly.

Jenny swallowed hard. She'd left the only way she could. Saying goodbye would have been too hard— not without making a total idiot of herself.

She wished he hadn't come.

"I don't like goodbyes," she said.

His hand drew a folded piece of paper from his pocket.

"I brought your check." He held it out.

Staring at it for a long moment, Jenny finally shook her head. "I don't want it."

"Why not? You earned it. I hired you to watch Jamie—which you did. You took very good care of her."

Jenny moved away from the door.

"Would you like something to drink?" She did not want to have her involvement with Jared or Jamie reduced to that.

She didn't want the money.

"Iced tea if you've got it."

"Sure."

She continued to the kitchen, glad for the respite. Her nerves were jangled. Her breathing erratic. She had spent days trying to forget and nothing had been forgotten. It only took one glimpse of Jared to prove that.

"Need any help?" he asked from the doorway.

She jumped and turned, almost bumping into him. Backing up to the counter, she shook her head, her eyes locked with his.

"I don't want to be any trouble," he said in a low voice, stepping closer, crowding her, brushing his fingertips along her arms.

He might not want to be trouble, but he was. Or her reaction to him was. Always had been.

"I'll bring it out," she said, hoping her knees would hold her up. If he'd only move away, go back to the living room.

"Something wrong?" he asked, raising one eyebrow.

She glared at him, dismayed to find amusement dancing in

his eyes.

"Why are you here?" she asked.

"I brought you the rocking chair."

"You could have left it on the doorstep."

"Is that what you would have preferred?" he asked, leaning closer.

Jenny put her palms against his chest, wanting to push him away, to give herself some room. But the instant she felt the solid strength of his body, his warmth, she curled her fingers against him, and held on.

His hands rested on her shoulders, brushed the hair against her neck, his fingers tracing patterns of fire and ice that had her forgetting everything except how much she longed to be swept into his arms. To have him kiss her.

"Jared?" she whispered. Was this the last time she'd see him? Had he come to say farewell to his family before returning to the U.A.E.?

She'd thought she'd been strong when she walked away last week, but she had doubts she could do so a second time. Not without giving herself away.

She wished he hadn't come.

"Jenny," he said softly and kissed her.

It was powerful and familiar. Without thought, her arms encircled his neck, and she opened her mouth to his sweet assault. Her body was pressed to every inch of his reveling in the spiraling feelings that were flying out of control.

He was all she ever wanted and the one man she couldn't have.

When the kiss ended both were breathing hard. At least she wasn't the only one affected, she thought, finally summoning the strength to push him away.

"Maybe staying for tea isn't such a good idea," she said, refusing to look at him.

She dragged a shaky hand through her hair and started for the living room. She needed time and distance, not more tantalizing kisses to point out what she couldn't have.

She walked to the rocker and pushed it gently, remembering the times she'd sat in it with Jamie. Remembering Jared sitting in it with the tiny little girl snuggled so trustingly in his arms.

"When do you leave?" she asked.

Somehow she had expected him to catch the first flight out once the cast had been removed. Maybe there was some of his father in him after all—a duty visit before taking off for the excitement of life in a foreign country.

"That depends on a couple of things," he said slowly leaning against the kitchen doorjamb. His hands were in his pockets, his attitude casual and non-threatening.

Except his very presence threatened her equilibrium.

"Such as?"

Despite her best intentions, she couldn't resist looking at him again. She could do this—she just needed to keep her distance. He wouldn't be long. Then she'd have the rest of forever to get over him.

He smiled wryly and ran a hand around the back of his neck. "I arrived in Whitney yesterday. Rented a car big enough for the rocker."

Jenny nodded. He wanted to see his family once more before taking off for who knew how long.

"Had an interesting talk with my father last night," he said.

"Oh?"

Despite knowing she should ignore any exchange of

confidences, she was curious. "About what?"

"He asked when I was returning to the Middle East. When I mentioned to him that I might be staying in the States, he seemed surprised. Then he danced around the issue, but finally asked if I was looking to get married. He said that time was passing and I wasn't getting any younger. When I said he was a fine one to tell me that given his views of marriage, he seemed totally perplexed. He hadn't a clue that his complaining over the years had left such a negative impression on me."

"What did he think it would do?"

"Actually, he didn't think at all. One of the first things he did after we talked was go to my mother to apologize for his unthinking comments over the years. He loves his family, Jenny. He would have liked to travel when he was younger, but he said last night that he wouldn't trade a single minute of family life for all the wandering in the world."

Jared shook his head. "He said some of his best memories were when Patti and I were children—the times we spent together. Playing ball, going to the beach, teaching us to swim. Even helping us out with algebra—which turns out to be hard for him."

"That must have made you feel better."

"It got me to thinking—well, actually, thinking more."

"Thinking about what?" Her heart was racing again.

"Thinking about life, how fast it can change. Jim and I were the same age. I could have just as easily been the one killed in the explosion. And what have I done?"

"Traveled a lot."

"So I have a few memories—but nothing to leave when I'm gone."

"I thought you wanted to be footloose and fancy- free. At

least you get to live your life just like you want it."

"The good thing about life is goals can change. Once one has been reached, it's time to make new ones."

Jenny longed to say something, but she couldn't. She could only gaze into his dear eyes and try to understand what he was trying to say. She refused to let her hopes rise that this conversation was heading somewhere she wanted.

"You brought sunshine and color and excitement into my life. It was barren when you left. I want you, Jenny. I want you in my life from now on."

He pushed away from the door and walked toward her. "I want you to marry me, Jenny."

"You never wanted to get married again," she said, stunned at the sudden turn of the conversation. "You were most adamant about that."

"Honey, we've been living just like we were married—except for the sleeping arrangement. I know how you decorate a place and I like it. None of that cloying lacy stuff Andrea used to fill up the apartment with."

"Hire a decorator."

"There's so much more. I know what makes you laugh, what captivates your interest and how mushy you can get over things. You have a genuinely kind heart. Mrs. Giraux adores you. You were patient and loving with her and with Jamie. And with me in my cranky moods. You're a terrific cook. We dealt well together, didn't we?"

Jenny felt a clutch in her heart—Jamie. How could she forget her? She swallowed hard.

"Dealt well together, is that all you want?"

He'd stopped by the rocking chair. Reaching out, he took her arm, drew her around until she stood right in front of him.

Taking both arms in his hands, he bent his head to see her better.

"I want nights of passion, lazy days reading the paper, long walks around the Quarter, and laughing times in the kitchen."

He'd said nothing of love. The omission was glaring.

"Well?" he said, folding her into his arms.

His gaze grew puzzled at her lack of response. But Jenny couldn't joyfully accept his proposal without love.

She'd promised herself.

She deserved it.

Gently she disengaged herself. "I'm honored you would want to marry me. But I—"

"Don't say no. Think about it. We were good together," he said quickly.

Almost desperately.

"I know this is a surprise. The entire time you were in New Orleans you heard how much I was against the institution. But even before I talked with my father, I knew I wanted you back."

"What about your job?" she asked, stalling. She longed to be swept up and away and never question a thing, but he had not said a word about love. She refused to enter into a loveless marriage!

"I'm transferring to the Gulf operations. If that hadn't been a choice, I'd quit and find something else. I'm not going to be an absent husband like Jim was. That's not what I want, Jenny. I remember what you said. I want to be with you during the week, spend weekends together. Be with you because you give me something I can't get anywhere else."

She stepped toward the door. "You've caught me by surprise," she said. Gripping the handle, she turned and looked at him. "I think we both need to think about this."

He still hadn't said he loved her, but the change was astonishing. Maybe he did and didn't know it. Maybe she should not refuse out of hand, but give him some time as requested.

The look of disappointment on his face stabbed her. But she was too emotional to think clearly. Holding on to the yearning for love kept her from blurting out her acceptance—no matter what.

"If that's what you want," he said coolly. Walking to the door, he stopped beside her. "Would it change anything to know I'm going to raise Jamie?"

She looked at him and all her dreams crumbled.

He was going to keep the baby.

And naturally needed a mother for the child. The reason for his visit became crystal clear.

It was all she could do to keep from bursting into tears.

"I thought you were taking her to the attorney to turn over to that private agency the morning after I left."

"I was. I did. At least, we got in the cab and headed that way. But the closer we got to Arthur's office, the more I questioned what I was doing. Then—she smiled at me and my heart just melted. She's my best friend's child. I can't turn her over to strangers. I don't know anything about being a father, but I'll give it my best shot. She's all I have left from Jim."

Clearing her throat, she tried to smile. "I'm glad for her sake. You'll make a great daddy. And you'll be able to tell her all about her parents when she's older."

"I thought you cared about her. About me."

"I do."

Oh, so much, she thought More than life. But she wanted

to be wanted that much for herself. To be loved and cherished for who she was, for how she alone could bring a completeness to a man.

Not as a substitute mother.

"Then?"

She shrugged, wishing he'd leave. Wishing for time to be alone and work through the pain his announcement had caused. To search her heart to see if she was strong enough to reject his offer, or if she loved him so much she could give up on her own dreams. Take what he offered and make do.

On the one hand she'd have her perfect family. On the other, could she live year after year knowing she had been married to provide Jamie a mother? Better to cut the ties now than suffer for decades.

"I'll have to think about it."

"There's nothing to think about" he said with a spurt of anger. "Either you love me or you don't."

"Love?" Her head jerked up. She searched his eyes and saw only baffled sincerity.

"What have we been talking about?" he roared.

"I thought you wanted a mother for Jamie."

"Guess again." He leaned his forehead against hers, gazing deep into her eyes.

"Love?" she whispered, almost daring to hope. Almost.

"Yes, love. I love you, Jenny Stratford. I didn't want it to happen. I didn't expect it to happen. I thought I was above all that romantic stuff. Now," he shook his head, rubbing it against hers, "I can't even imagine my life without you in it every day. You shattered my ideas of a carefree nomadic life. Now I want to see your smile, touch your skin, feel your caresses, breathe your scent. I haven't thought of anything since you left except when would I get to see you again, be with you again, hear your voice, touch you. I want you to want me the same way, with the same intensity!"

"I thought you wanted a mother for Jamie," she repeated, feeling confused.

Feeling hopeful.

Releasing her grip on the doorknob, she linked her arms around his neck. He quickly pulled her into a tight embrace, resting his cheek against her hair.

"That would be nice. But if that's a problem, we can go back to plan A. I thought you loved her enough that we could take her and then have a few of our own to round things out. You don't want her to be an only child, do you?"

Jenny shook her head, tears starting to build.

"You love me?" she asked.

"Yes, Jenny, I love you. Care to say that to me?"

She nodded, tears slipping down her cheeks. "I have since that first night I think."

He laughed shortly. "You kept it hidden. Except maybe from Mrs. Giraux. She urged me to get up here right away. Not that I needed any urging. As soon as I got the doctor to remove the cast, I was coming if I had to walk. But she's the one who convinced me I had a chance. She's going to be as doting a grandmother to our kids same as my mom will be."

He kissed her.

And all doubts fled.

Jenny wasn't quite sure if she was on her head or heels, but she didn't care. She was where she always wanted to be.

He ended the kiss far too soon.

"Will you marry me?" he said softly.

"What about your job? How long before you return?"

"I have to return to Abu Dhabi for a month or so, to close

up my apartment, train my replacement. But I've already put in for a transfer to the home office. And it's been approved."

"For me? You did that for me?"

"Partly, sweetheart. Partly, I did it for me. I have nothing in the U.A.E. All I want and need is here."

He tightened his embrace.

"I want to be home every night to see you and Jamie. I want to hear about the kids in your class that drive you nuts and help you find a way to deal with the burping boys. I want to touch you in the night, know you are there. I might even spring for a house in the suburbs and a dog."

She swallowed hard, trying to hold back the tears, but her eyes were swimming.

He tilted her face, studying the tears and the tremulous smile.

"I hope those are happy tears?"

She nodded, reaching up to pull his head down for another heartfelt kiss. She'd never been so happy in her life.

Jared loved her!

Together over the years ahead they'd forge her perfect family. But she'd already found perfection in his arms.

"I love you," she mumbled against his lips smiling as she cherished being in his arms.

Jenny finally had her very own family.

—The End—

Did you enjoy this story?
If so you may enjoy **Mail Order Bride** or **Because of You**

More books by Barbara McMahon

The Harts of Texas Series
Rebel Heart
Tangled Hearts
Reckless Heart

Cowboy Heroes Series
Blue Bells on the Hill
Cowboy's Bride
One Stubborn Cowboy
Crazy About a Cowboy
Never Doubt a Cowboy
Cowboy Marshal
Summer Cowboy
Second Chance Cowboy
Movie Star Cowboy

Tropical Escape Series
Island Rendezvous
Come into the Sun
Island Paradise
Destination Romance Boxed Set

Rocky Point Series
The Family Next Door
Rocky Point Reunion
Rocky Point Promise
Rocky Point Hero

Elite Security Mystery Series
Trusting Jake

The Ultimate Billionaires
The Cynical Sheikh
Falling for the Sheikh
A Sheikh of Her Own
The Unforgettable Sheikh

Other Books
A Soldier's Christmas
I'll Take Forever
Jared's Promise
The Paper Marriage
The Christmas Locket
The Banished Bride
Cowboy Charade
The Cowboy's Special Christmas
Mail Order Bride

www.ingramcontent.com/pod-product-compliance
Lightning Source LLC
Chambersburg PA
CBHW071303250626
47159CB00004B/1290